Serenade Our End

A Novel

Ian Gill

Cover art by Ava Levine

ISBN: 978-1-7376643-0-7

"Where there is no hope, it is incumbent on us to invent it"
- Albert Camus

Prologue

Run. I have to run. In my current situation it is my only option. As I rush across the leafy ground, my thoughts are focused on my children. If I am unable to survive, they will have no mother. How could I possibly leave my children with no mother? The thought is too difficult to bear, so I push it from my mind. I weave through the white and black aspen, my pursuer falling farther behind, but I am not yet in the clear. I take a sharp left turn in an attempt to throw him off. My stamina is beginning to fade, but he appears to be going strong. I notice a gap in a rocky outcropping just ahead, and as I approach, I leap with my full strength. My body effortlessly flies through the gap, and I land gracefully on the other side. This does not mean that the chase has ended, so I turn and continue my sprint. I continue running until the gap in the rocks is out of sight, obscured behind the endless emerald green Aspen leaves.

I collapse onto the ground; my flight having taken an inordinate amount of energy. I remember that my brush with death at the hands of my pursuer does not excuse me from today's foraging duties. If I am where I think I am, I need to head north until I see the large boulder forking the road, then take the path on the left to the most promising area. I rise from the earth and begin my journey, this time at a brisk jog, nothing like my earlier sprint. That is when I see it. Out of the corner of my eye, I notice him standing there. I launch my body forward as fast as I can, but I am too slow to fully avoid his projectile. Its pointed tip slashes through the flesh on my back, but fortunately it does not become lodged within me.

Thoughts of my children and their perfect, small bodies guide me through the pain. That's right, I can't die. It would mean death for them as well. I resume my sprint, albeit hampered by my wound. Even so, my pursuer is far slower than me, although he has substantially more stamina. I need to use my speed to my advantage, find an alcove of some sort that he would move past once I got out of sight. With every footfall the wound on my back pulses, spitting blood. Despite my pain, I remain grateful that it only grazed me.

I notice a river to my left, and hoping that he can't or won't swim, I plunge into the cold rushing water. I quickly make it to the other bank of the thin river, thankful not to be overwhelmed by the current in my weakened state. I have a choice. I could run parallel to the river, or I could go straight and up the hill facing me. If I follow the river, he might see me if he decides to follow it too. However, I have never been on this path, so I know not what lies on the other side. Considering how dire my situation is, I decide to travel up the hill and hope that it does not lead to a ledge or dead end.

I push forward, my legs burning from the exhaustion of such a long sprint coupled with searing agony from my injury. But the physical pain pales in comparison to the thought of leaving my children alone, so I know that giving up is not an option. As I reach the top of the hill my eyes are greeted by the welcome sight of a slow incline down. I charge forward, running across the cracked pieces of concrete from an abandoned road. On the other side of the road, I see a derelict house, complete with a broken fence. I decide that the fence might be something worth hiding behind, so I try to hop over it.

Instead, I stumble over the fence and land painfully on the other side. Getting up after this fall seems entirely in the realm of fantasy. I wait to recover my strength before I resume my flight, but the blood continues to pool on the grassy ground, and I feel no stronger. I force my thoughts back to my children and feel something incredibly deep down, a primal yearning to live. It screams in my mind and echoes throughout every molecule of my body. I am filled with the strength to rise once more in search of safety.

When I get up, I see a very unfortunate sight: my pursuer standing in the distance on the other side of the fence with a bow poised, aiming right at me. I try to move, to escape him as I had before, but this time I am not as lucky. The arrow pierces my chest, bringing unbearable pain. He had shot from fairly far off, so I limp behind cover before he can make his next shot. The blood continues to spill out from my wounds, my strength dwindling with each drop.

Even in the face of all this pain, surrendering to my pursuer would be a shame upon my children, so I limp forward. It seems like forever but is probably closer to thirty seconds. Even in my hazy state I hear my pursuer approach from the rear. I hear the creaking of his bow, the whoosh of the arrow as it flies to deliver me it's baleful purpose. I even feel like I hear the rending of flesh as the arrow pierces my skin, but this is most likely just my imagination.

I crumble as my legs give out, leaving me an immobile hunk of meat. This is it. For all my running, my pursuer has gotten the best of me. I stare at him as he leisurely walks towards me, knife in hand. On his face is a look of grim solemnity; he takes no pleasure in this. This is his task, just as mine is to feed my children. Even as I look death in the face, I feel not fear but regret. Regret that I could not escape, and sadness that my death will most likely be followed by the deaths of my young ones.

He kneels beside me and lightly brushes his hand against my neck. Even though I would have appreciated a quick death, his attempt at comfort was not lost on me. The second arrow pierced my lung. I feel my breathing begin to strain and my head falls to the ground. I turn up and see the knife hovering above my neck. Time seems to slow as the knife is lifted, reaching a serene apex. The sunlight glints off the metal, the leaves rustle above me, and the birds still chirp as they always do. The blade falls with astonishing speed and by the time it lodges itself in my neck, all my periphery fades away. My vision darkens and I can almost see my two children approach from behind. As the warm blood paints my skin, my thoughts begin to jumble and then fade, replaced by a stark emptiness. I close my eyes.

And do not open them again.

Ezra

June 2

I kneel in front of the dead doe, feeling the usual sorrow that comes with a kill. Some part of me resents the world for how it pits all living creatures against each other, but there is no use wasting my energy raging against the immutable. I pull my hunting knife out of her neck, my gloved hands slick with blood. I wipe down the knife against the ground until all the remnants of blood have mostly vanished from its shiny surface. My own deep blue eyes stare back at me from the blade's reflection.

Now that the poor thing is dead, the most dangerous part of the hunt commences. Dirtying the clean knife once more, I carefully cut off a square of the doe's skin near the center of her torso. I place the knife beside me and use my hands to slowly extract the now detached skin from the body of the doe and fling it as far away as I can. I pull off my left glove and lay it down next to me. With my ungloved hand, I reach into my backpack that I have slung around my shoulder and pull out a canister of water that I had filled up at the stream this morning. I douse both of my gloves until there is no blood remaining on either of them. I then loop my arm out of the strap of my backpack and lower it to my side. Still wary of my gloved hand, I search for my scalpel with my left. I grasp its metal handle and yank it out from the clutter surrounding it. The rows of scabs on my left hand have mostly healed, so even if I make a mistake and get blood on the wound I would most likely be okay, but I am not taking any chances today. After all, if I'm wrong there won't be any do-overs.

I drop the scalpel on the ground and proceed to pinch a clean section of the glove between my index finger and the thumb of my ungloved hand. I cautiously slide it off and lower it next to the other glove. I then pick up the scalpel using my recently degloved right hand. Like clockwork, I move onto the next step, placing the edge of the scalpel behind the knuckle of my ring finger, as the spaces behind my index and middle fingers are still healing from past hunts. I quickly push forward, slicing off a thin layer of skin. After putting down the knife, I grab the layer of skin and place it on the patch of uncovered flesh that I had carved out of the deer. Just as my hopes begin to rise, the color of the sliver of skin changes and slowly, it begins to bubble. As more time passes it shifts from a solid, to a sludge, and finally to a liquid

"Well shit," I mumble quietly.

I take a step back from the doe and any equipment that had any contact with its blood. My first priority is to ensure that I cover the wound that I just made on myself. I dig through my bag for the medical box, finding it quickly. I open the white and red plastic box and find a large band-aid to place over the top of my hand. I carefully put my hands back into the gloves. Visions of Melchior's teachings play back in my mind. As long as the doe's flesh or blood doesn't enter my body, I have nothing to fear. This is by no means the first time I have dealt with an animal infected by Sin, but it still scares me every time I do. I realize that I still haven't removed the arrows, so I try to pull both out, twisting as I go. Both arrows come out, but one of the heads is too badly damaged to be reused. I decide to head back to the river I passed through earlier during the chase so I can wash the gloves, the knife, and the arrow thoroughly enough to feel safe with them.

I give the gloves a deep scrub in the flowing river water. Confident that I have washed off any traces of the animal's blood, I leave after about a minute. On returning to the doe's corpse, everything is just as I left it, save for a large increase in the amount of deadly blood that has seeped into the ground. I put the now empty canister of water, the scalpel, and the medical box into my backpack and place my hunting knife back in its holster. The animal's glassy eyes gaze at me.

"Don't worry," I whisper.

Hopefully, Quinn found some food because I doubt I will catch another animal before the day is done. He would say I am wasting my time. Regardless, I take a trowel from my bag and slowly begin to dig. The doe isn't that large, so its grave shouldn't take that long to dig. Based on how low the sun is in the sky, I anticipate that it is around 4:30. I can't say I regret killing the doe, but it feels so wasteful to have ended this life for no reason. There is no way to screen for Sin while the animal is still alive, but it still makes me feel like shit. The dirt speckles my pale skin as I dig. Covered in dirt or not, I certainly felt dirty.

After a decent amount of digging, the grave is finished. Making sure not to touch the bloodied parts of the doe, I grab its two hind legs and drag it into the freshly dug grave. I replace the dirt until the ground is flat over her. At least this way her nutrients won't go to waste. Once I double check to make sure all my equipment is in my bag, I start walking north toward the camp. My legs ache from the fruitless, long day's journey. My mind wanders during the monotonous travel. This place really is beautiful, the aspen, the rushing wind, and clear sky. Tarnished by Sin no doubt, but beautiful nonetheless.

I notice red and blue markings on a rock deeper into the forest. I remember Melchior said that they denote different paths for climbers before the Rapture. It still blows my mind that not too long-ago people would climb not for survival, but for fun. I guess that's what happens in a prosperous society.

My thoughts then drift to the fact that I've been seeing fewer and fewer animals in this forest every day since Quinn and I got here. I hadn't seen anyone else besides the people from the village, but I feel like the supply of game shouldn't be falling this quickly. I don't know how long we can stay here if we can't find enough food. We should probably be okay for tonight though - I think that we still have some leftover venison jerky from the last hunt. It is still discouraging that I couldn't find anything today.

After a long walk I finally see some familiar terrain. I travel up the hill that's facing me, hop over the decrepit stone wall, and take a left at the big tree. The sorry camp ahead has two lightly padded bed areas with sleeping bags and a fire pit filled with charcoal between them. I lament Quinn's unwillingness to just stay in the village, but there isn't much convincing him once he has set his mind on something.

He isn't back yet, so it seems like I'm going to have some time to myself. I reach into my sleeping back and sweep my hand around until I feel it. I grab its hard cover and pull it out. The Pearson Learning Algebra II textbook feels comfortable in my hands. It always has, from the moment I pulled it out from the rotting stack of books in that collapsing school. Whenever I open the book, I'm transported back to the decaying classrooms, and to thoughts and dreams of what might have been, in another reality far from this one. Perhaps that is why I do it so often. I open it up to page 237 and start reading the section on composite functions, content in the simplicity and objectivity of math for those sparing moments.

Quinn

I've always loved mushrooms. Most other gatherers pass them by out of fear that they might be poisonous. But with the right eye, mushrooms can be the difference between survival and starvation. As I spy a group of Porcinis, my stomach grumbles just at the thought of them. I need to avoid. getting too excited, since I have no idea whether they are safe. The good thing about fungi is that since they are all connected, if I test one mushroom for Sin, I am effectively testing all the mushrooms in the immediate area. I pull my knife out of my belt and slice the Porcini in half. Using the point of the knife, I lightly pierce the skin on the pad of my pinky finger. I hold my finger above the Porcini for a few seconds until a droplet of blood leaks from the wound that I had just made.

The red ichor lands on the slice of the Porcini. Those few seconds start to stretch as I wait for a reaction or lack thereof. Thankfully, the gods of chance reward me by selecting the latter option as the blood remains intact after about ten seconds. This is a good batch, with about seven Porcinis here at the base of this tree. I slice each one of them at their thick stalks, ensuring I cut as low as possible so there is the maximum amount of mushroom to eat. I put them in the Ziploc bag I use to hold everything I gather. Today has been fairly successful, so the bag is packed with a hearty mix of wild berries, mushrooms, as well as some nuts. I never could bring in as much as Ezra could with his hunting, but at least I am consistent. I like that.

As my thoughts drift to Ezra, my eyes widen, and the corners of my mouth start to rise before I force them back down. Not now. I can daydream about Ezra later, but I still have work to do today. Then I recall that Ezra asked me to check one of his nearby snares. I stand up, having finished my job, and begin walking west until I see the split rock. I am vaguely familiar with this area, so I have the basic idea of how to reach the place he was talking about.

I hadn't ever checked the snares before, as that falls into hunting, which is always Ezra's job. While I feel that I should be able to do it without a problem, there is an uneasy feeling in my stomach as I make my way to the split rock. I look around at the trees and other foliage that surrounds me to try to distract myself. It looks beautiful, but it feels… less so.

My thoughts are interrupted when I see a concrete road up ahead. It's cracked and falling apart, but people often use the old roads rather than risk getting lost in the forest. As I approach, I crouch to make sure that I won't be spotted by a passing traveler. Even though I have almost never seen anyone pass through this area, I take the utmost precaution. The most dangerous thing in this world is not Sin or starvation, but people.

People are a lot like mushrooms. Plenty are wonderful and bring comfort and happiness to those around them. Others, however, are toxic and will ruin anyone they come into contact with. The distinction between people and mushrooms is that with people it is impossible to tell which are poisonous and which are not. The seemingly most kindhearted person might stab their companion in the back if it meant more food. Before the Rapture, the stakes were lower; if a person betrayed you, it might mean a broken relationship or some lost money. Now is a very different time, trusting the wrong person could leave you dead.

I rehearse these lines in my head as I watch the empty road to ensure that it is truly so. After about 45 seconds, I decide that it is safe. As I sprint across the cracked pavement, I hear a rustle to my right. I stop suddenly and turn around. About 20 feet away from me, I notice a shaking bush; it's almost as if there is someone on the other side rubbing up against it. I watch for a few seconds to see if it is just the wind, but the shaking continues, and the wind is silent. I reach behind my back and draw the revolver I have holstered. I point the weapon at the trembling bush, my arm quaking with adrenaline.

"Hey, look man I don't want to hurt you just come out," I shout at the bush.

The shaking stops. I have no idea if I am prepared to do what's necessary in the worst-case scenario. I think of Ezra and his perfect smile, praying to no one in particular that I get to see it again. Suddenly, the bush bursts open. Charging towards me comes a lone Bighorn sheep. I dodge out of its way, and it continues its dash down the road. Relief like no other floods my body. Without much delay, the relief begins to turn to embarrassment. What was I thinking? What kind of person would just stand there and shake the bush? I hate the road.

I hop over the guardrail on the other side of the street. I continue making my way to the split rock, mentally admonishing myself the whole way through. At least Ezra wasn't there to see my stupidity. Once I reach the rock, I take a left and then head about 60 paces forward. Hanging in the triggered snare trap is a small brown rabbit. While I would never consciously admit it to myself, a part of me hoped I would find only an empty snare.

I approach the squirming little creature. It wants to live so badly. I too want to live, which is a desire that unfortunately comes into conflict with that of the rabbit. I draw my knife and raise it to the rabbit's neck. How do I even do this? Melchior only ever taught me the stuff I needed to gather because that has always been my job. I guess this seemed so second nature to Ezra that he didn't even bother to tell me what to do. Logically, I have no problem with ending its life. This is the food chain, it's how this fucked-up world works. But as I stare into the little creature's eyes, I simply can't kill it. I stand there for a few seconds, just looking at the rabbit, then at the knife, then at my arm, then back down to the rabbit.

Abruptly, I put all my force behind the blade and slice forward. The rabbit falls to the ground and after a moment of confusion, scampers off as fast as it can. The sliced snare hangs in front of me. I try justifying my actions by thinking that they are just a result of my fear of Sin or my ignorance of how to kill the rabbit painlessly. I don't really believe either of these, but they are comforting mantras to repeat when I think of the event.

I pick myself up from the pool of shame that I had been swimming in for the past few minutes and trudge east towards the camp. On my way, I fantasize about what my life would have been like without the Rapture. I would have gone to a normal school, gone to college, gotten a job, lived without fear of being murdered at any moment. I don't know what job I would have had specifically, but I know I wanted something to do with writing. Huh, that's funny, now would have been the time that I would have been applying for college. In my fantasy I imagine that I would have met Ezra at school and that we would go to the same college and live a happy life together. But all fantasies must end, and as I approach the camp, this vision of a more pleasant existence fades away.

Chapter 1 - Ezra

June 2

I hear him before I see him. After all these years with him, I've come to know the sound of his footfalls. I put my textbook back in my sleeping bag and stand up to greet him. Quinn smiles as he sees me and gives an excited wave. I wave back, incredibly happy to see him. As he gets closer, he calls out to me:

"Howdy there, stranger!"

"Fancy meeting you here."

I wrap my arms around his tall shoulders, embracing him in a deep hug. After a moment, we release each other and sit down on the logs on each side of the fire pit.

"So tell me how your hunt went today?" Quinn inquires.

"I got a deer, but it had Sin."

"You were careful right?"

"Quinn, you know that I always am."

He raises his hands up in defense.

"I know, I know, I'm just checking."

"You're always so overprotective," I add with a smile. It's so cute.

"What can I say, I can't help it."

"Well, what about you? Did you find anything?"

"I harvested a good batch of Porcinis over in the western area."

"Excellent. It's good that to have something new."

"Oh, another thing. While I was crossing I-80, this

Bighorn sheep jumped out at me while I was in the middle of the road."

"A Bighorn sheep? Over here? That's strange."

Shaking his head shamefully he notes, "It scared the living shit out of me."

"Poor baby, did the wittle sheep hurt you?" I coo.

"I swear to god it was startling."

"Sure."

"It was!"

"Mhm."

Quinn sighs, "You know you wouldn't be able to get away with teasing me like this if you weren't so cute."

I smirk.

"I know."

He suppresses a smile and stares at the ground to try to maintain a straight face.

"You know that's not going to work right?"

He breaks out into a grin then chuckles, "Yep."

"Anything else exciting besides the attack of scary Bighorn sheep?"

In a deadpan tone he retorts, "Well yes, actually, I was assailed by giant scorpions with laser eyes."

"Of course. That's perfectly reasonable. Very frightening."

"Nah, it's not like they were Bighorn sheep."

We both break out into laughter. Looking into his eyes, seeing him smile, it's the best thing about this ragged existence of mine.

"In all seriousness, today was pretty average. I did check that snare you asked me to, but it looks like someone else snatched whatever it caught."

"Ah, that's unfortunate. But we should still be grateful that we have enough to eat for tonight."

He might be telling the truth, but I wouldn't bet on it. Ultimately it doesn't matter to me. He's not a hunter after all, so if he missed a kill, it wouldn't really be his fault.

"Yeah, for sure," Quinn replies, seemingly eager to change the subject.

"I'm going to get the fire going so we can boil those Porcinis. Sound good?"

"Sure, go ahead."

I begin collecting tinder and dry wood I find lying on the ground. I wish I knew what's going on inside of his head. After all these years, all this time together, I still don't know. Whenever I'm left to my thoughts, they inevitably begin to involve him, or more specifically him and me. If I wasn't so preoccupied with trying to survive, I don't know how I would function. But then again, if I wasn't so preoccupied with trying to survive, I probably would have asked him by now. Fuck Melchior for designing it like this. I can't live without his skills, and he can't live without mine. If I ask him and he doesn't feel the same, I have to live with that awkwardness forever. My desire to avoid that situation is still larger than my desire to ask him. Slightly.

Before I know it, I have collected all the materials that I need to start the fire. As the camp enters my view, I see Quinn furiously scribbling away in his journal, lit by the small electronic light that he found a few weeks back. If only I could read what's in there. I quickly expunge the thought from my mind. I would never invade his privacy. My focus returns to what's in front of me. Quinn already has the pot and the water ready, so all that is left is to get the fire going.

"Boo," I call to him as I approach.

"Terrifying," he comments without even looking up.

I place all the wood and tinder I'm carrying in the fire pit. Quinn has the flint and steel out, so I kneel in front of the pit and strike a fire after a few attempts. Quinn puts his journal down and moves to put the pot over the spit that we had in place above the fire. He pours the water into the pot and plops in the Porcinis along with some other vegetables that he gathered. Now we just have to wait. I sit back on my log.

"The stars are pretty. Aren't they?" Quinn says with his eyes on the sky.

"Indeed, they are. I suppose it's one small benefit of this dark world we inhabit. Twenty years ago, I bet you we could barely see any stars where we are right now."

"Luminations of the distance become brighter when all other lights fade," he observes somberly.

"Okay there Nietzsche."

"Come on, you can't tell me that this world hasn't gone completely to shit."

"Oh yes, the world has gone to shit, but that doesn't mean it's hopeless."

We have had this conversation, or some variation of it, dozens of times. We always know exactly how it goes, but we do it anyway. Maybe we just like the sound of each other's voices.

"Think about all the terrible shit that people have done to us over the years. The grand experiment, human socialization and civilization, it's over. There is no coming back from this. When humanity faced its greatest challenge, it revealed something supremely ironic: a total lack of

19

humanity. An empty reservoir of compassion. Humans are a selfish, brutish, and vile species."

"People have always been vile and selfish, Quinn. They have also always been kind and generous. Each person in our village would be better off killing each other and stealing everything there. But they don't, whether that's because they care about each other or simply don't have the ability to kill others, they work together. Yeah, sometimes people work together to do fucked up stuff, but the fact that people can still cooperate at all in such a dysfunctional environment is a sign that not all hope is lost."

"Obviously not all cooperation is lost, but I would say that's only because of familial ties. Three or four families live in that village, and they have known each other since before the Rapture. Once those time-honored agreements fade away, the only compacts that remain between people will be agreements to steal from and kill each other."

"Well, they let us in, didn't they? They had no relationship to us, but they still sheltered and aided us."

"Only because we helped them fend off that raider attack when we first came here. It's tit for tat, noy altruism. The ultimate issue is that there simply isn't enough food for human cooperation to be a real possibility. Melchior told us that tens of thousands of years ago people wandered around in small groups and hunted large game. When half of the food you find is inedible, it makes existing in groups as a whole a near impossibility because the amount of labor that you can muster can't make food appear out of nowhere. The land is already straining to support the village."

"Sin strains human relationships, that I won't deny. But the thing is that Sin is going to continue to spread until there is no food left anywhere. This means for humanity to have any hope of long-term survival, Sin has to eventually go away. So that means that your argument is based on people themselves being monsters," I argue intently.

"I wouldn't say I think all humans are monsters. I would say that Sin has done something so damaging to the human psyche that almost all positive relationships have been corrupted. Large groups can only exist by stealing from smaller groups. This is a fact of life in today's world. Even if by some miracle Sin disappears, over a decade and a half of such a violent hierarchy won't be easily dismantled. Even our neighbors view us with distrust, and we reciprocate. It sucks, but it's the truth.

"Sin has not damaged the human psyche. If anything, it has just shown our resilience. Despite Sin, people still work together. Groups still form and people are still social. This is why the world is not doomed. If Sin suddenly went away, these groups that already exist would grow and develop into civilizations. If there were no groups at all and people lived completely alone or with their families, then maybe I would concede to a hopeless world, but it's not so. Even in the face of the ultimate de-socializer, humans are still social."

"There's no point in arguing about this while our positions are so fixed. We still have plenty of time left to live, so we can pick this up later, once we have new arguments for a change."

"That's probably a wise decision."

The two of us recline so we can stare at the twinkling stars. The forest is quiet, with no noise but the crackling fire and the rustling of leaves overhead. It is a calm summer night, and Quinn and I intend on enjoying it to its full potential. We gaze in silence, but it is not an awkward silence. Instead, it springs from the fear that any noise or movement might shatter this moment. If only it could have proceeded uninterrupted, but after a few minutes the spell is broken when Quinn says:

"I think the food is done."

We don't have any plates, so we use two scavenged spoons and scoop out the mushrooms one by one. We hadn't eaten anything since morning, so we're ravenous, eating up the Porcinis in less than two minutes. They are delicious, not by any virtue of their own, but rather because food always tastes better when you're starving. After we finish, Quinn pulls out his Ziploc bag that holds some wild berries. He wordlessly offers them to me. I grab a few and pop them in my mouth. Even after eating these, I am still by no means sated. We still have some jerky left over from the last kill, but it would be wasteful to eat it tonight just to placate my appetite.

"Can you believe that years ago most people didn't even have to concern themselves with finding food? They just went to huge food stores and traded for whatever food they wanted. No slaving away the entire day just to try to make sure you don't starve come evening," Quinn says, eager to continue our conversation.

"It is pretty crazy how different things were, yeah. But also, I wouldn't trivialize the challenges people faced back then. Sure, a bunch of them had food security, but that doesn't mean they didn't work hard. The human mind will set a baseline for life expectations, making you happy when it's above it and unhappy when it's below it. We just have a substantially lower baseline, but to say that the lives of pre-Rapture people were easy is an oversimplification.

"I suppose I agree with that. It still just feels like they didn't know how good they had it. I guess it's just that you only realize how good things were when you don't have them anymore."

"The idea that you are getting at rings true for us. We have way more than your average wastelander in that we have each other and that we were taught the skills to survive. We should be grateful for what we have, even in this mess of a world."

"Mhm..."

"Wastelander. It's interesting that we call each other wastelanders. Sure, human infrastructure may be falling apart, but nature is as strong as it has been in years. The planet is regrowing, slowly but surely, back to a world that existed before she was put under the crushing boot of humanity. Maybe it's a wasteland for us, but it's a utopia for the hundreds of thousands of other types of life on Earth. Environmentally, at least where we live, it's only a wasteland in a very human sense. We used to control all this land, but now, we are just passengers in it, the only land we truly own being tiny patches where minute towns develop. The land is no longer ours, so we call it a waste."

"And you called me a philosopher! It's probably just that wasteland was popularized by pre-Rapture, post-apocalyptic media, so once the apocalypse actually happened, it was just the name that people jumped to. I don't know exactly how pervasive that kind of media was since obviously we don't remember being that young, but from what Melchior said there certainly was a lot of it."

"Yeah, that's possible, but I feel like what I said is true as well, even if it's not perceived on a conscious level."

"Could be, could be."

I empty the water from the pot and place the spoon within it. I leave it at the edge of the camp.

"I'll take that down to the stream tomorrow morning and clean it," Quinn says.

"Awesome, thanks!"

It is probably only around 9:30 but considering that we always have to get up early, we decide to get some shut eye. We tidy up the camp and crawl into our sleeping bags under our tents.

"Goodnight! I love you!" I call to Quinn.

"Sweet dreams! I love you too!" He responds.

Clinging onto those words, I drift into the comforting void of sleep

Chapter 2 - Quinn

June 3

The dull glow of the sunrise creeps into my eyes. My sleeping bag is warm, comforting, and pleasant while the outside world possesses none of these qualities. I want more than anything to lie in its embrace forever. But as much as I want this, today, like every other day, I force myself out of bed and take a good stretch. I grab my jeans that lie next to my bed and quickly put them on. Ezra's still sleeping soundly, so I decide not to wake him until I return from washing the pot and the spoons. Another day in paradise.

I take my backpack and stroll out of the camp, still half asleep. I hate mornings. My surroundings are serene, something Ezra might actually enjoy. On my way to the stream, I notice some edible berries that are hanging from a bush. Before I get my hopes up, I test them for Sin, quickly pricking my finger and letting a drop of my blood fall into the meat of the berry. The blood fails to disintegrate, meaning that the berries are good to eat. I reach into my backpack to pull out the Ziploc but remember after a few seconds that I don't think I put it back in the bag last night. Shit. I take a few of the berries with my hands and decide to just hold them for the time being. Once I clean the pot, I will throw them in there. I continue my walk towards the stream, pleased that I have something sweet to offer Ezra when he wakes up. As I hike, I think back to last night. Speaking with him, being with him, it's all that I look forward to in this wasteland. Soon enough, I break through the thick trees and gaze upon a wide-open field of grass where the stream lies.

My eyes widen. My hands unclench, letting the berries fall to the ground. I stand in shock for a few moments, unable to fully grasp the gravity of what I'm seeing. Past the tree line on the other side of the clearing, I see three large pillars of black smoke extend up into the boundless sky. There is only one place that smoke could be coming from: the village. I turn around and start sprinting back to the camp as fast as I physically can. Ezra and I need to get out of here. There is no way a fire like that is an accident, no there is only one possible source for this. Gunshots echo behind me, practically filling in the rest of my thought. Raiders.

The burn emanating from my calves would be unbearable in almost every other circumstance, but right now I could take anything if it meant getting back even ten seconds faster. I didn't even consider why the raiders were there or what they wanted. It's always the same; time after time people kill each other over food and land. My focus is laser sharp. Each footfall I make is incredibly deliberate, and my ears are on edge for even the slightest disturbance. I make it back to the camp and prepare to shout to wake Ezra up, then reconsider in case there are any raiders nearby. I stop in front of Ezra's sleeping bag and see that he has already begun to squirm awake from the sound of my steps.

"Ezra, you need to wake up now, there are raiders in the village, and we need to get out of here."

He sits up immediately. He gets out of his sleeping bag and says, "We can't just leave those villagers to die. We have to help them."

"Are you out of your mind? What are we supposed to do against a whole band of raiders? Plus, it's not our job to help every poor soul in existence."

"Think about Jamie. She will almost certainly die if we do nothing, and she's probably alive and terrified right now. We can't just let them kill her!"

"You don't know that she's even alive -"

Ezra interrupts me and states, "Her family has weapons. They will probably stay holed up in their house for a while. We have to go. Now."

"Fuck it. Fine, let's go."

We are putting ourselves in terrible danger for what is likely a hopeless cause, but I know Ezra would never be able to forgive me or himself if we didn't go. On Ezra's face lies a look of pure determination. I love him. I never want to put him in any dangerous situation, but today I know that he just must do this, and I would never let him do it alone.

"Who knows when we will come back here, so take everything that's essential," I remind him.

"Got it."

I pack up my sleeping bag and some other stray items lying around the camp. I had put my rifle right next to my sleeping bag for safe keeping, so I snatch it and throw it over my shoulder. I check to make sure that the revolver at my hip is still ready. In truth, I am genuinely scared for what is about to come. I can't let Ezra die. I just couldn't function without him, literally and figuratively. Perhaps it may be unreasonable, but I resent the raiders for putting us in this position more than I do for the actual harm they've caused the village. I wrap my fingers around the grip of my weapon and squeeze as hard as I can.

"Alright, you ready?" Ezra asks after we had both finished picking up our belongings.

"Yeah, let's go."

We start off at a jog, as we don't want to be too exhausted by the time we make it there. I consider asking Ezra if he still thinks there's hope for humanity but decide not to waste my breath. We will talk about it after this. There will be an "after this." We make it to the clearing before the stream where we can easily see how the smoke has bloomed even higher into the sky.

"Oh my god," Ezra says under his breath.

"Come on," I say, motioning forward.

We keep rushing forward, the determination in Ezra's eyes burning even brighter. What if, when we get there, everyone is dead? How will he respond to that? No, I can't think like that. The villagers are tough. I'm sure they have put up a serious fight. I shouldn't think about this, since speculating is useless to me right now. I just hope this isn't going to be like what happened before.

Ezra, somehow sensing my apprehension, tells me, "Quinn, it's going to be fine. We aren't going to charge them head on, and we have dealt with situations like this before."

Too out of breath to respond, I just give him a quick thumbs up. We're getting closer to the smoke with each passing moment. I don't know why I'm so scared. I'm not afraid to die. I never have been. It's hard for a life like this to provide that kind of eternal motivation. Maybe I'm scared for Ezra, or maybe I'm scared of suffering. As much as I would love to continue psychoanalyzing myself, the smoldering village in front of me is demanding my full attention.

Ezra and I are kneeling upon a hill that has a good overhead view of the village. There are four main housing areas, all of which are torched. Bodies both familiar and unfamiliar are strewn across the ground. We see about fifteen raiders meandering about the camp, looking for goods or survivors. Most surprisingly, we see a band of about four cars parked near the village. How the hell did they get those? Where did they get gas for them? It used to be abundant in the old world for sure, but today you would be hard pressed to find any.

"Quinn, look, top right corner of the village behind the remains of the Reynolds' home."

When I look, I see three chained up villagers, with a raider standing behind them. I take a closer look at the villagers and notice that one is a little girl. I can't make out if it's Jamie, but it might be.

"Alright what's the plan?" I ask.

"The only thing we can do here is try to free those three. We got here far too late to be able to try to help anyone else. I say we follow the tree line until we get close to them. Then we jump out, try to incapacitate the raider holding them, undo their restraints, and run back off into the forest. Hopefully they won't come after us if we don't kill anybody. Sounds good?"

"Alright got it."

We start following the tree line, making sure to stay low as we aren't completely obscured from view. As we approach the captives, we still can't make out their identities since their backs are turned to the forest. The raider, though - we can see him clearly. He's a middle-aged man, pretty tall, about 6' 2" maybe, and incredibly muscular. He has a pistol holstered on his leg, but no larger firearms. Even though I expect people to act like this, on some level I just don't understand. If everyone just worked together, I'm sure we could produce an outcome that's better than this. How don't they see that? Quinn and I reach the edge of the forest closest to the raider, slowing down to reduce noise as we approach.

The raider is only about fifteen feet from us now. Ezra quietly approaches the man from behind while I aim my revolver at him, just in case he suddenly turns around. As Ezra gets within five feet of the man, he charges. Just as the man is about to yell, Ezra slams the butt of his rifle directly into the man's jaw. The raider is knocked off his feet, landing flat on his back right where he used to stand. He is out cold. Ezra immediately walks up to the captives, brandishing a knife so he can cut their restraints. I start walking towards them and as I do, an abject horror fills me. The raider, who is in fact not out cold, draws his pistol and points it at Ezra in one smooth action. I sprint towards the man, hoping that I can stop him somehow. I have to. I can't let this happen. Time seems to slow while the man sits up and stabilizes his aim. I watch him apply pressure to the trigger, and mere moments before I reach him, he finishes his task.

Click.

No bullet is ejected from the chamber. Realizing his mistake, he flips the safety off and prepares to try again. But now, I'm already upon him. I dive into him, giving him a jab to the gut with my elbow as I land. Our faces are only inches apart as we struggle to try to seize control of the weapon while we wrestle on the ground. I look into his eyes and see a burning desire to live. I know he sees the same when he looks in mine. Both of us have our hands on the gun, pushing it to try to get its deadly barrel facing our opponent. Holy shit, this guy is strong. I'm using all my might to move the gun, but the weapon is slowly moving towards me. What should I do? I can't win, I'm going to-

Bang. Bang.

Warm blood begins to pool around my stomach. It is only after a few seconds of panic that I realize that this blood is not my own, but rather that of my adversary. I look up and see Ezra pointing his weapon at the now-dying man.

"Check him to see if he has car keys cause they're coming for us now. I need to finish untying the captives."

I take the man's gun and put it out of his reach. He's dying, but he isn't dead yet. I climb over him and start running through his pockets. The determination in his eyes is replaced by pure hatred. It feels so wrong, searching a still-breathing man, but I have no other choice. I feel a small plastic bag in his left pocket, so I pull it out. There is a strange key in the bag that is unlike any that I have seen. It must be the car key. I open the bag, but I feel something other than a car key as I reach in. I take out a small, square piece of paper. Gazing on it, I find my worst fears realized. It's a photo, with the man holding what seems to be his two infant daughters.

I throw it on the ground and reach in the bag once again for the keys. My fingers clasp around them, and I yank them out, my mind still focused on what I have seen. Logically, I recognize that he is clearly in the wrong here. He was threatening innocent lives, and we had a right to subdue him. And if we hadn't, those villagers would be dead. They are worth more than him, right? I believe all of these things. Yet I still cannot shake the feeling that we have done something terribly wrong.

"You got them?" Ezra yells.

"Yeah, come on, let's go."

Ezra calls me out of my mental spiral and reminds me that we still have to escape. I stand up from the half-corpse and turn to Ezra. I see that he has already freed the villagers, their ropes now scattered on the ground. The villagers themselves are nowhere to be seen. We are running towards the cars when it hits me. Neither of us knows how t-

Bang.

A bullet crashes into the burning rubble next to me. Around 200 feet behind me stands a man scowling and reloading his hunting rifle. We take a left and weave through the burning wood on the ground, breaking line of sight with our pursuer. Just ahead of us stands three dirty white trucks. Luckily, no one is standing guard. I hear a small burst of gun shots come from behind me, although they sound somewhat far off. I fear at any moment we may be struck down, but Ezra and I make it to the truck on the far left unharmed. I push the key into the hole in the door. It doesn't fit.

"Shit. Let's try the other one," I say to Ezra.

Two bullet holes appear in the truck I am standing by, but I don't even bother to turn around to see who fired them. We dash over to another truck and try the key. Now is the moment of truth. It slides smoothly in. I turn it quickly and throw the door open. Ezra hops in and I quickly follow him, shutting the door and ducking so I can't be shot through the window. I see a spot near the wheel where the key could go in, so I put it in and twist it. The steady rumble of the engine gives me confidence.

"Well, here we go!" I shout as I slam my foot on the gas.

Chapter 3 - Ezra

June 3

"Don't crash okay, idiot?" I say to Quinn.

"Huh, really didn't think of that."

The cracked and rocky road is causing the car to bounce up and down violently. Quinn is trying to drive as fast as he can, but these roads are too old to handle the speeds of their prime era. We turn the first corner after the village, taking a deep breath as it vanishes from view. Still, I unsling my rifle and poke my head and arms out the window in preparation. I watch the corner for a few seconds, waiting for more white trucks to come flying around the curve. After a few seconds of nothing I almost gain a modicum of hope, but then I remember that there's no way that they will let us go. My thoughts are confirmed as two trucks come around the bend.

I aim at the tires of one of the cars. I wrap my finger around the trigger and pull. The recoil pushes me back against the frame of the car, but fortunately it seems that my shot has paid off, as one of the cars starts to slow down. I duck back inside the car and reload the hunting rifle. I hear the clang of bullets as they pound the chassis of the truck. At this point sticking my head out would be suicide. From the sound of their car, I can tell that they are gaining on us. We have a lot to learn about driving.

I look around for some grand trick, something from the action movies that Melchior used to show us, anything that could save us from the raiders. But there is nothing, no pipe bomb to incinerate their car, no tree that can be conveniently knocked down in their path with just a single shot. They have numbers and experience, while all we have is a burning desire to make it out alive. Right now, it's only a matter of time until they shoot out one of our tires, meaning game over for us.

Just as we round another bend and break line of sight for a moment, I peek back out the window. I point my weapon to where the truck's wheel should be as it turns. As the car pulls into sight, I make eye contact with its passenger, who evidently has the same plan as me. It's a race to fire then. My body acts faster than I thought possible, instincts and training driving me.

Bang.

We both fire. I see my opponent's car swerve and slow down, with its right tire completely busted. I wait for a few seconds to see if there might be another car chasing us, but the road remains clear.

"Shit!" Quinn yells.

I barely have time to see what's going on before Quinn swerves sharply right. While throwing myself back into the cabin of the truck. What caused the commotion? Two rusting skeletons of what used to be cars blocking the upcoming road. They are sitting right after a curve in the path, so we couldn't have seen them far in advance. The front of our truck crashes into the rusting guard rail on the side of the road. My panic intensifies when I see that below the guardrail is a 20-foot drop.

The truck enters freefall and pitches forward. If this is how I die I hope that it will at least be quick. As we hit the bottom, my ears are assaulted by the roar of rending metal.

My head hits the dashboard hard, but I remain conscious. Then a second impact occurs as the car flips onto its roof. The metal bends: the roof slowly gets closer to me. Just when I think the ordeal is over, the car begins to roll, repeatedly for more times that I can count. When stillness finally comes, I don't believe it at first. I turn to Quinn to see if he is okay. He appears limp, but also doesn't have any major wounds besides a few scratches.

"Hey there, stranger," he mutters weakly.

"Quinn, are you alright?"

"I'm fine, now how about we get out of here?"

Both of us hang like bats by our seatbelts. I lean forward a bit and release mine. Fortunately, most of the force of the fall was shifted to my back, but my neck will probably be sore tomorrow. A lot of me is going to be sore tomorrow. Quinn does the same thing, leaving us both sitting on the interior of the roof. The doors have been too badly mangled to open, So Quinn begins kicking on the window. One. Two. Three. On the fourth hit, the already damaged window shatters. We both crawl out, trying our best to avoid getting cut too badly by the broken glass.

After I exit the wrecked truck, I see that we landed in a downhill patch of mud, causing us to roll out of sight of the road. Even though it made for a bumpy landing, it is probably the only thing that saved us from the vengeance of the raiders. From first glance, we appear to be situated in something of a sinkhole, but as I looked more thoroughly, I noticed that the walls are concrete. I turn around and see a completely rusted, decrepit car. That's when it clicks: this must be an underground parking garage, opened up by a sinkhole. The muddy hill leading up to the surface looks too steep to climb, and even if it wasn't, there are raiders waiting on the other side.

"Hey look there's a door over here," Quinn shouts from across the open space.

"Quiet!" I whisper-shout back at him.

I make my way over to where he is standing and see a dark passageway past a concrete door frame.

"Should we go into the ominous hall?" I ask.

"If this was a horror movie the audience would probably call us stupid right about now."

I can barely believe that he cracked a joke only about a minute after he almost died, but I think it helped both of us dissociate from the bleak reality of what might have been. Quinn takes out his electric lantern and turns it on as we walk through the doorway. There isn't any ornamentation or anything to indicate what this passage might have been, but as we make it to the end, we see the word "Ichthys" in big lettering with the subheading of "Third Branch." As we make it past the lettering, the hall opens into a grand underground structure. We notice a directory of sorts erected in the front of the chamber. I see that there are three floors to this building, with each floor having different titles. Floor one is listed as administrative, but floors two and three have something strange going on. It seems that they used to be divided up into subsections like "Excavation" and "Governmental Affairs," but all of these tags have been covered up with new ones saying, "Lilith's Egg Research." The same goes for the third floor, where these different labels are replaced with "RIAA Research."

"Well, I suppose the only way to go is up, yes?"

"Guess so."

We walk along the wall of the chamber until we feel it suddenly turn a corner. Using Quinn's light, I see that this is because of the staircase that lies past this little inlet in the wall. We carefully make our way up the stairs, making sure to avoid any cracked steps or flimsy handrails. This staircase only takes us to the second floor. As I walk onto the second floor, I see the wall next to me curve upward, suggesting that the room is spherical. I move forward and identify a railing of some sort. I couldn't tell from below because of the limited light, but it seems that this chamber is an atrium-type structure.

"What do you think this place was?" Quinn asks me.

"Honestly, I have absolutely no idea. It seems like maybe it was a government thing, but even then, why are the floors renamed? And Lilith's Egg? What the hell is that? That sounds like something out of one of those Asimov Sci-Fi books Melchior let us read. I always hated those."

"Yes, Ezra. I'm very aware. We have discussed this multiple times."

"Hey! Let me express my hatred in peace."

"Whatever thee command, good sire."

We notice a door titled "Dr. Canum's Lab." While it almost certainly won't lead us out of here, some level of human curiosity drives me to open the door. I take out my own light and tell Quinn to keep looking for an exit. The room contains rusting metal devices and large instruments. It even has a computer! It's been a while since I've seen one of those. It looks to be in pretty good condition too. I doubt anyone has been down here since whatever caused the owners to leave in the first place. I go to the main desk in the room and start rummaging around, looking for anything that might be useful. In the leftmost drawer, below a derelict stapler, I find something completely unexpected: A stack of laminated e-mails.

"Hey Quinn come over here I found something interesting."

"One sec!"

I take the top email out and start to read. It takes me longer than it should to decipher the text of the well-worn document, but eventually I recognize the gist of the first few sentences.

```
12/15/06
To: All
Re: Break Room Fridge

Hello co-workers, I hope you are all
having a pleasant day; I just wanted to
give you all a little reminder. As per my
last email, the break room fridge is NOT a
communal space. You can ONLY eat what you
bring, so don't just take something from
there because it looks good. I'm only
saying this because...
```

That is not the most interesting relic of the pre-Rapture era, but I guess it proves that bickering has always existed, apocalypse or not. I stop reading halfway through as Quinn walks in.

"What is it?"

"I found some pre-Rapture emails, wanna read?"

"Sure," he responds.

I hand him the paper, and he starts reading.

"Forget all the other weird things about this place, a new mystery has appeared. Who is stealing from the break room fridge?"

"Alas it seems that we shall never know."

"Unfortunate."

I take the rest of the email stack out of the desk and pass them to Quinn. He starts flicking through them rapidly.

"These are mostly just routine or maintenance emails like the first one. Wait. There's a time skip here; it goes from May of 2007 straight to October of 2007. The summer is missing."

"Wait, that can't be right, they couldn't have been sending emails after the Rapture."

"I mean, clearly they were. This seems like an important facility so they must have had some sort of backup power. But even more than that, this Dr. Canum guy was still laminating his emails after the world ended. Wonder what he's like."

"What is the last email in May?

"It's just a notice that the lab is closing early on Friday for Memorial Day weekend."

"What about the first email in October."

"Look."

```
10/13/07
To: All
Re: Confirmation
```

Team Sigma has done a thorough investigation into the Egg. By tracing the spread of the outbreak, they determined

that it was the cause of RIAA being
released. As I'm sure you are all aware,
this makes it our responsibility to fix
this issue. All of you have lost family
members, coworkers, or lovers, but now is
not the time to give up. The rest of the
world depends on us here at Ichthys...

The email was ripped after that. This one wasn't
laminated, but it was saved from destruction by the ones
above it seems.

"Holy shit,"

"Ezra, this is huge. This place I mean..."

I shake my head in disbelief. "Are there any more
emails after that one?"

"No, this is where the stack ends."

Wordlessly, we both walk out the door and start
looking for another room to search. The thoughts running
through my mind are impossible to describe. I had taken Sin,
or RIAA, whatever that stands for, as something that was a
fact of life, like space or gravity. I don't know how or why
those forces of nature exist, and I assumed I never would.
Sin was thrown into that category as well, but now, for the
first time in my life, I have a chance to find some answers.
Quinn and I rummage through the labs of Dr. Burling, Dr.
Carlton, and Dr. Kruczynski, but are unable to find anything
of value.

"All these rooms seem pretty destroyed. I found
another staircase right before you called for me, let's head
up, okay?"

"Got it," I reply.

The concrete staircase is almost identical to the one from earlier. Quinn walks ahead of me, and as he takes a step forward, the concrete chips and he stumbles backwards. The second I heard the crack; I already began reaching out my arms. I brace myself for the impact, but the force of his fall almost knocks me down anyway. Luckily, I shifted my footing in a way that let me stay standing. As he lies in my arms, I look directly into his eyes, forgetting myself for a moment.

Quinn cracks a slight grin before softly saying, "Hello there, Romeo."

My heart flutters for a moment, but I recover, smoothly replying, "Well I hope not. That would mean we both die in the end."

"Let's skip that part. Now how about you let me back up?"

"Oh yeah, whoops," I say as I push him back onto the step.

As I walk my heart rate starts to settle from the chaotic events of the past hour. How can I be making jokes after I just killed a man? I can't think of it like that. I just did what I had to in order to ensure the people I cared about got to live. I shouldn't dwell on what I have lost and what I have taken. What's done is done and it's up to me to make the best of the future.

We continue making our way up the stairs, quickly arriving at the third floor. From this floor, the curvature of the chamber is even more apparent. We brush by a door where most of the letters have faded away, with only "Dr. c o   lab" remaining. I try to open the door, but when I attempt to turn the handle, it doesn't budge. Seeing the futility of my efforts with the handle, I move on to body slamming the door a few times, but still, it continues to hold strong.

"In here," Quinn calls to me from a few doors down.

"Coming."

I move in through the open door titled Dr. Shelby's Lab. Quinn stands hunched over the desk in the center of the room, reading a sheet of paper.

"Is that-"

"Yep."

I get closer to the document, and I see that time has ravaged all the text on the center of the page. Only the beginning, most of which we had already read, and the last few sentences remained

```
10/15/07
To: All
Re: Confirmation
```

Team Sigma has done a thorough investigation into the Egg. By tracing the spread of the outbreak, they determined that it was the cause of RIAA being released. As I'm sure you are all aware, this makes it our responsibility to fix this issue. All of you have lost family members, coworkers, or lovers, but now is not the time to give up. The rest of the world depends on us here at Ichthys to defeat this monumental threat to the human race. The remnants of the US government are directing everyone with any sort of

scientific background in biology to start
work...

The second through fifth branches
will be working as auxiliary facilities to
support the first branch, which will be the
body synthesizing the counteragent. We have
lost communication with the sixth and
seventh branches in Japan, but we believe
they are working on a counteragent
independently. We are under the assumption
that the eighth branch in Germany is out of
commission due to a message we received
from them before global communications went
down indicating that they are abandoning
their posts. We have heard nothing from the
Ninth Branch in France. All staff please
begin work. Good luck and Godspeed.

We stand there for a moment, taking in the
information we just read: someone was working on
developing a cure for Sin. To me, Sin had always been like
that story of Pandora's box that Melchior used to tell us
about. But now, that underlying assumption about the word
had changed in an instant. On the wall of the lab, we see a
map of the US, pointing out all the branch locations. As we
walk up, I pull my journal out of my bag and flip to an open
page, I begin drawing its location. Next to it, it gives the city
and address, which I write down as well. I also make sure to
take that letter and stuff it in my bag.

Quinn stands next to me and says, "Well it looks like
we'll be heading to South Bend."

Chapter 4 - Quinn

June 3

201 Chapin St, South Bend, IN 46601. This is where we might actually find some answers, and hopefully some people who know what happened to the world. Better yet, they might have a cure developed - maybe it just hasn't made it this far west yet. In this dirty, decrepit room, Ezra and I have hope, real hope, for the first time.

"Well, we better keep searching the other rooms around here before we leave," I say to Ezra as he scribbles away.

"Sure, good plan."

We open all the drawers in Dr. Shelby's room, but we find nothing else of any real value. There are still two unopened labs on the other side of the atrium, so we make our way over there, leaving the door to Dr. Shelby's open. Unfortunately, the path connecting this side of the atrium has collapsed from years of neglect.

"Shit, I think the exit has got to be on that side too," I say while shaking my head.

"Well, I guess we only have one option then," Ezra states before sliding into a sprinting position.

I don't even have time to react before Ezra takes off.

"STOP!" I yell at the top of my lungs.

Ezra manages to grab the railing of the walkway, slowing him to a stop just before he reaches the missing chunk.

I walk up to him and say, "Ezra please, please don't do that again. Do you understand how dangerous that was? What if the walkway breaks away on the other side, what if it's longer than you think? This isn't some fucking action movie."

"I'm sorry it's just, I don't know, don't you feel insane right now? Like I can't even believe what we just saw."

"I do, but we can't let it get to us. Come on, let's look for a ladder."

"I think I saw a room called 'maintenance closet' on the other side of the stairs."

"Let's check over there then."

We walk back to this maintenance closet, and inside it we find a long, extendable ladder. I kneel to search for any other items of value, but all I find are some pairs of rusted pliers and a hammer. It can't hurt, plus I have some extra space in my pack, so I throw the hammer in.

"See Ezra, this is a much better solution than just jumping and praying."

"Yeah, yeah."

We walk the ladder over to the gap, extend it to the max, and stand it straight up. I release the ladder, letting it fall forward, creating a horizontal bridge across the gap.

"Now for the fun part." Ezra says to me

I only sigh in response. He strolls up to the ladder, kneels, and makes his way across the ladder by sliding his knees across its bars. He reaches the other end of the gap with relative ease. Okay. I can do that. Easy.

"Come on hurry up!"

"I'm coming!"

I follow Ezra's exact footsteps, hoping that might grant me some sort of protection. As I kneel down in front of the gap, I stare into the black abyss below me. Quinn, chillax, it's a 40 foot drop not Cthulhu's lair. I look forward at Ezra as I make my first few steps on the ladder, trying to keep myself firmly tied to my destination and not what is below me. I hear the ladder groan under my weight. Hopefully, this didn't become brittle during those years left alone in the maintenance room. I count my steps remaining until the end. Five, four, three, and I see Ezra's outstretched hand ready to pull me onto the platform. My count continues, two, one, and thankfully, zero. Ezra pulls so I am solidly on the platform. Near the end there I really expected something to give out, but it seems like I've gotten lucky.

"I never knew you were afraid of heights," Ezra jokes.

"I'm not afraid of heights, I'm afraid of 30-year-old ladders being the only thing between me and those heights."

"Hmm, ladders, I guess I'll just add it to the list with Bighorn sheep."

"You are never going to let that go, are you?"

"Nope."

We make our way towards the labs. When we reach them, we notice that the nameplates have been removed. The door is rusted shut, but after a few good body slams, we get it to open. Inside, we see charts and tables and all sorts of data strewn about the lab. I suppose that this is RIAA research, so it does make sense that they would have all this stuff. The charts make no sense to me, full of strange number and letter combinations. I think Melchior said those were called chemical formulas, but I wasn't sure.

"Do you have any idea what this says, because I am absolutely at a loss," Ezra asks.

"Lemme look."

What Ezra shows me is something like a list of chemicals, things I had never seen before, with the heading of Ardenium-1 enzyme. It seems like they were figuring out what Sin was made of.

"Can you believe that? I mean Sin isn't like an abstract quality or divine retribution, but rather just something biological, like you or me."

"I guess, I never really thought it was divine retribution, but it's good to know for certain that it isn't."

We scour the room for something we can make sense of, but we find nothing discernible. Realizing that those raiders might come back to make sure we were truly dead, we are filled with a new sense of urgency. We leave the room and take the stairs that are next to the lab. These are far longer than the other stairs, making me think that they exit above ground level. At the end of these stairs, we find a big metal panel. With our combined weight, we force the panel open. The room we open into is not a boring office or non-descript hallway, but rather a movie theatre.

"Well, this is weird," I say to Ezra.

"Yeah, and also how did we not notice this movie theater as we drove in?"

"Maybe it was overgrown with vegetation?"

"Must be."

Ezra walks up to one of the seats and hops on to it.

"Imagine watching a movie on this big of a screen."

"I'm sure it's nothing like that tiny screen from way back when. But anyways we gotta go. Raiders, remember?"

"Oh shit, that's right."

He exits his seat, and we walk down the aisle of this collapsing theatre. The doors open into a hall filled with movie posters preserved in their glass cases. On the left we see a poster for "Harry Potter and the Order of the Phoenix." Melchior mentioned that movie to Ezra and me when we were little, specifically how he never got to see it. I realize that that series will remain eternally unended, as if humanity does recover, Harry Potter will most likely remain forgotten. Even more concerning is the fact that everyone on that poster is dead by now. In fact, all the people in every poster in this hall are probably long gone. Armed with this knowledge, the theater feels less like a piece of nostalgia of days I never had, and more like a hall of the dead.

Thankfully, we come to the nexus of the theater relatively quickly. The place where they used to sell popcorn now has only empty shelves, and the room of the ticket booth collapsed due to time's wear.

"This is why I hate going into ruins. It's creepy," I say to Ezra.

"You're creeped out now? Not in the underground lair where the government did secret experimentation?"

"Maybe it was just the adrenaline, but I think the difference is that down there was already a weird and creepy place, derelict or not. This theater, on the other hand, was meant to be a place of fun, but now it's just… empty. Like something has been lost that you can never get back."

"I think that something definitely has been lost, but this goes back to what I said earlier, because it was only lost for us. The plant life, the fauna, has made this place their home, they gained what we've lost."

"True, but that fact doesn't fix the feeling."

"That it does not."

We arrive at the glass doors that lead to the strip mall outside. I try to open the door, but nothing is ever easy, so of course it doesn't budge. I turn around to look for something to pry open the lock and see Ezra behind me poised to throw a brick from one of the collapsing walls.

"Come on, get out of the way."

I roll my eyes and say, "Yes, master."

I move back behind Ezra and wait for him to throw the brick. Let's hope there's no one nearby. The glass shatters with a loud crack. We stand there for a while with our weapons drawn making sure that no raider is going to come sprinting at us. After about twenty seconds of silence, we move forward. Ezra steps through the broken glass door first and I follow him, but as I do, I feel a sharp pain above my ankle. I look down and see that I cut my foot against a protruding shard of the glass. Shit. I stop for a little bit to look down at my wound. Ezra turns around to see what is taking me so long and sees the blood dripping from my ankle.

"Quinn, oh my god, are you okay?"

"Yeah, I'm fine, don't worry, it's just a scratch."

Ignoring my statement, Ezra proceeds to come up to me and pull the first aid kit out of his bag. He takes some bandages and wraps them around the wound.

"We have to go. We don't know how far behind us they are."

"Alright, alright."

He doesn't have enough time to fully finish dressing the cut, so as we begin to walk droplets of blood fall on the path. The exit to the theater is on the second floor of this small strip mall, so we have to make our way down some concrete stairs. This time I make sure to watch my footing more carefully, so I don't take a tumble down the steps. I look around at the rest of the building and see stores with incredibly generic names like Quick Stop or Shoes-4-U. This place was so obviously a front.

"When I was looking at that map it showed that the most direct route to South Bend is going to be following Interstate-80. Otherwise, we will almost certainly get lost," Ezra says to me as we reach the bottom of the staircase.

"No no no no, I do not want to be traveling along any road, much less an interstate."

"Quinn, we've got no other choice. It doesn't sit right with me either, but it's the only way."

"Fine but know that I'm not happy about it."

"You don't have to be. Anyways, I-80 should be due north of here."

The road bordering the mall is full of cracks, just like any other road around here. It's enclosed by trees on either side, which would be kind of pretty if being out in the open didn't terrify me. We walk silently along the road, internally digesting the events of the morning. It still doesn't even feel real. Wait. I completely forgot to ask.

"Ezra, I never saw... was Jamie one of the people we saved?

He looks up at me, makes a slight frown and says, "I'm sorry."

"Oh."

"It doesn't mean she's gone. I didn't see her body either. She might have gotten away."

51

"Yeah," I say quietly.

While Ezra is right to say that she easily could have gotten away, my monkey brain interprets our inability to find her as a mark of my failure. She was good and pure, but this rotten world ripped her away. And I couldn't stop it. She was just an innocent kid and yet... I feel so many conflicting and complex emotions. The life I have grown used to has been suddenly ripped away from me, but I am also being presented with an opportunity to do such unimaginable good.

"I just don't understand why those raiders did that. The villagers had nothing. What did the raiders gain by risking their lives to kill them?" Ezra asks.

"Hmm, what have I been telling you this whole time? Humans are rotten to the core."

"Quinn, philosophy aside, they must have wanted something. Only a very select group of people kill for killing's sake."

"My best guess is that they were worried that there were too many people in the area, so they decided they needed to take us out to protect their food supply. I mean, you and I have seen the decline in food sources recently."

"It's just so wrong. I wish they could recognize that."

"Me too."

I'm not going to keep rubbing it in, but it is no doubt clear to Ezra, as it is to me, that regardless of the reasons, the brutal action of the raiders proved my point. Humanity sucks. But the attack on the village is still too raw for both of us. Before long, we see a sign for I-80. When I make it onto the road, I find that it's very wide and open. I do not like this. However, the two of us continue our walk-in silence, luckily not running into any other people or Bighorn Sheep. We walk for hours, letting the day slowly drift by. Fallen exit signs periodically litter the asphalt, a consistent reminder of the realities of this world. In many places the guard rails bordering the road have completely rusted away, which isn't too much of a travesty as I doubt they were getting much use anyway. To spice up the monotony, Ezra leaps up onto the concrete barrier separating the two sides of the road and attempts to balance on the ledge. He is moderately successful, but after a few minutes he misplaces his foot and comes tumbling down. By the end of our walk, the soles of my feet are burning from the long day's travel along the hard pavement, so when I see the sun begin to set, it's a relief.

"Well, we should probably make some sort of camp now, shouldn't we?" I say while trying to hide my slight panting.

"Yeah, let's go off the road here," he replies, clearly attempting to hide his panting as well.

We head into the forest and out of sight of the road. After we are a suitable distance away from the road, we take a well-deserved seat on the ground.

"Do we have any leftover food we could eat since we didn't hunt today?" Ezra says to me, clearly alarmed by the realization that we might go hungry.

"Yeah, I think we have some leftover jerky, but really we probably should have hunted today - we shouldn't go into our reserves unless we absolutely have to."

"We needed to put some good distance between us and the raiders, we absolutely had to."

"I guess."

We take our sleeping bags out of our packs and lay them down next to each other. It's probably only about 8:30, but we are out of it from the long day of travel, so we decide to just munch on the leftover jerky and call it a night.

"Goodnight! I love you!" Ezra says while lying in his sleeping bag.

"Goodnight! I love you too!"

As I drift off into sleep, I gaze up at the starry night sky, praying that my dreams are full of worlds far, far away.

Chapter 5 - Ezra

June 6

"I'm telling you, they used to have video games where they *pretend* to hunt," Quinn says to me, clearly exasperated.

"I know that you have no reason to lie here, but I just don't believe you. Why the hell would they have a video game that simply imitates something that's mostly waiting? Like I get wanting to satisfy a primal desire and all, but they had war games, and don't those sate two primal desires at once?"

"I don't know why they existed, I don't know how they existed, I just know that they did. I saw the cover of one when we were passing through this store a couple of months back."

"Fine. But you're on thin ice."

The road ahead of us is completely empty, and the noon sun hangs in a cloudless sky. It's a nice day. In the distance, I see a road sign coming up, one of those that used to tell drivers where the nearest rest stops were off of the interstate. Normally I don't pay much attention to these, but today for some reason my focus is drawn to it. Below a McDonalds and above an Arby's reads a promotional for the Colorado Air and Space Museum. It states that it's only one mile away from the upcoming exit.

"Hey Quinn, maybe I'll believe your video game claim more deeply if you decide to go to the Air and Space Museum with me."

"What- huh how do those things even relate? And what Air and Space Museum? Where would we eve-"

His eyes flicker to the sign, igniting a look of recognition to flash on his face. He tries to give a disapproving look, but I can see him suppress a smile. This battle is already won.

"No, I mean we can't, we have to go to South Bend. Or what if some raiders turned the Air and Space Museum into their camp. We just don't know. It's too dangerous."

I look at Quinn and give him the biggest puppy eyes that I can.

"Pleeeease."

"Ugh, fine you know I can't say no to that, you little demon."

"Hey, I'm not little, I'm 5'7."

"Still little to me."

"But-"

"Shh there's no winning here."

Eh, you win some you lose some. We take the exit when we reach it and find ourselves traveling along this quaint little road. There isn't anything to either side of us, and if I remember correctly, there won't be until after the museum, because the fast-food places were farther away. After a few minutes of walking, the place comes into view. In the front, I see a fighter jet, shrouded with vines and other plant life.

"That's a major downgrade for him, going from demon of the skies to decoration, and now all the way down to the lesser half of a potted plant," Quinn says.

"Hey, don't judge him, he's just going through a rough patch right now," I respond, suppressing a giggle.

56

The building itself has a very modern and geometric style. It is entirely square, with its exterior being largely stainless steel, interspersed with glass panels, many of which have shattered by now. The entrance to the facility used to consist of a beautiful glass door, but now, like many things, it has been smashed to pieces. We walk in through the door frame, this time careful enough so neither of us cuts an ankle on the remaining shards of glass. Upon entering the building, I see an old biplane hanging above me, suspended by some rusted metal cords. I feel Quinn's hands around my arms as he starts to slowly pull me away.

"Maybe let's not stand under the precariously hanging heavy object?"

"That does sound like an excellent plan."

In front of us we see an empty registration desk.

I go up to it and say, "Uhh, yes, hello. I would like to purchase two tickets please?"

After a moment passes, I turn and say to Quinn, "Wow the service here is terrible, isn't it?"

"Comedic genius at work here."

"I'm glad you recognize it."

To our right and left we see two escalators, one labeled "Air" and the other labeled "Space."

"So, good sir, who way would you like to go first?" I ask.

"Let's do air first, go sequentially, ya know?"

"After you," I reply, gesturing to the stairs.

We walk up the stationary escalators, this time pleased that neither of us has to worry about a piece of the stair breaking off, causing one of us to take a rather unpleasant tumble down them. I consider remarking about how people in the past were so lazy that they needed machines to do their stair climbing for them, but it was a different time. Making fun of them for what seems to be ridiculous to us isn't really acknowledging the larger context here. Circumstances build human behavior, so saying they are at fault for a commonality of a time they lived in is not wise or brave, but ignorant.

At the top, the first thing we see is a big sign with the title "The History of Flight." We seem to be on an upper-level balcony of sorts. There are exhibits over the ledge below us, so it must connect down there at some point. On the floor there is a white line with arrows coming out of it. Quinn and I follow the line for a few feet until we are above a part of the line that has the year 1783 marked in red lettering. Around us are panels that have information about why this year was relevant to aviation. Ahead of us we see a few more years with their corresponding panels.

Quinn begins to read the panel aloud, "On September 19, 1783, Pilatre De Rozier launched the first hot air balloon ever invented. From this moment onward, humanity would become permanently entangled with the heavens above us, pursuing better, faster, and bigger ways of traveling through it. Pilatre's hot air balloon, a replication of which can be seen to your-"

"Come on, let's skip to the jet engine. From what Melchior told me, those look absolutely amazing."

We stroll through the airships section, stopping briefly to look at a miniature model of the Hindenburg on display. After that comes the biplane, and then the propeller planes. All around us are hanging models of said planes, but we are too scared to walk off the path and go under them because we never know how strong the wires holding them are after so many years.

"I wonder how many planes are still flying today" I ask.

"Probably very, very few, considering that new fuel can't be produced. But we don't really know what it's like on the other side of the world. Maybe they found a cure for Sin and now just relax flying around in their planes."

"That's a fun dream."

"It sure is."

"Hey look, it's 1939. I think that's around when jets were invented."

We reach the panel and once more Quinn begins to read aloud, "On August 27, 1939, the first jet aircraft ever to be produced, named the Heinkel He 178, took off from Rostock, Germany. When the war broke out five days later, the jet engine would come to be a major part of the Nazi and eventually Allied war efforts."

"Yikes."

"Yikes indeed."

"That it was, let's maybe skip forward a little bit to a less horrible story of innovation?"

"Sounds like a plan."

The year we end up skipping to is 1969. Keeping with our previous structure, Quinn reads aloud once more.

"On March 2, 1969, the Anglo-French Concorde took its maiden flight. The supersonic passenger plane was one of the first of its kind, capable of ferrying passengers across the Atlantic in a fraction of the time it would take a subsonic plane. Moving at speeds of over Mach 2, this machine is truly a wonder of human engineering. Multiple reasons spurred joint development of the Concorde by Britain and France, ranging from economic interests to competition with Soviets, who were also producing their own version of the Concorde at the time, known as the Tu-144. On the panel to your left, you will see a more detailed history of the development of the Concorde, while on the panel to your right you will read about the Concorde's commercial history."

"That's wild. Can you believe that we used to travel faster than sound? And the sheer amount of people that had to come together to accomplish such a task it's just mind boggling."

"I can already sense how you are going to turn this into a 'humans are inherently cooperative blah blah blah' moment.'"

"You know me too well."

"I mean I already see the argument you're going to make, and it is a strong one. Everything in this room is a testament to the human ability to work together and to cooperate. But I would say that the reasons that people cooperated were only out of self-interest or hatred. I mean look at the Concorde. A huge reason for why they built that was to out-do their rivals. And the jet engine, while not directly invented for war, almost certainly wouldn't have had the funding to be produced without war existing. People worked together for sure, but it was just for a salary or against a common enemy.

"But I don't think that was the whole story. I think that many people worked for the goal of advancing human capabilities and knowledge. It shows how people put aside their personal rivalries with other innovators and worked with them to make something as amazing as the Concorde. It's that spirit that proves the togetherness of humankind."

"Maybe let's just enjoy the planes rather than philosophize about them?"

"Sure."

The Concorde amazes me more than everything else I've seen in here. It could travel an unimaginable distance in just three hours, the time it takes to walk just a couple miles. The world must have been just so much smaller back then.

"I wonder about all the planes that would have been made if Sin never happened," Quinn says.

"There probably would have been some pretty cool ones, but that's one of the smaller casualties of Sin."

"True. Do you wanna go over to the Space section now? I feel like we've gotten the gist of this area, plus we shouldn't stay here for too long."

"Alrighty."

We walk back the way we came, go down the stalled escalator, and up the one on the other side. At the top of the escalator, we find ourselves on a balcony like the one on the Air side, however, the floor doesn't seem to be accessible, but rather just a place to hold the tall rockets that we see on either side of us. There is also a guiding line marked with years starting with 1944. We head up to this first exhibit, but while I wait for Quinn to start reading, he instead says:

"This is another Nazi one - maybe wanna skip it?"

"Yeah, that sounds like a good plan."

We move on to the next exhibit, based in the year 1957. Once we arrive, Quinn begins to read.

"In 1957, the Soviet Union launched the first man-made satellite, named Sputnik, into space. This satellite was about the size of a beach-ball and orbited the earth every 98 minutes. Its launch on the similarly named Sputnik carrier rocket catalyzed the Americans to develop their own space program, as they did not want to fall behind their rival. The signal that Sputnik would emit as it passed over the US was a constant reminder to the government and the people that they failed. As we see in the coming years, America does not take this humiliation lightly. To learn more about the Sputnik satellite, read the panel to your left. To learn more about Soviet rocketry at this time, read the panel to your right."

"I bet that there are probably some satellites left from before the rapture still orbiting us. Melchior said that they used satellites to talk to anyone around the world instantly."

"I guess those satellites up there are relics of a time when humanity was better. But like everything else in this world, they'll crumble and decay with us."

"Hey, don't say that! We have hope for the first time in a great while. We may just discover a way to salvage this human race, or at least find someone who can."

"We do have hope, but hope isn't a guarantee. We have no idea if they are still alive, let alone if they have been successful. If we assume the worst, we can't be disappointed"

"Or we could just enjoy the hope we have right now."

"To each their own."

"Hey, I want to go learn about the moon mission. Can we skip to that?"

He nods his head, and we walk through the forest of rockets ahead of us until we reach the year 1969.

"1969 was an eventful year for the aerospace world, wasn't it?"

"Yeah, it was, but come on, start reading. I want to hear."

"On July 20, 1969, Man took his first step off planet Earth and onto another celestial body. Motivated by tensions with the Soviet Union, The United States began investing large quantities of resources into its space exploration department, NASA. The culmination of these years of R&D and testing was the Saturn V rocket. Standing at over 300 feet tall and 33 feet wide, the Saturn V was the largest spacecraft of its time. It was on this Saturn V rocket that the crew of Apollo 11, Michael Collins, Buzz Aldrin, and Neil Armstrong, took off from Kennedy Space Center on July 16. Over the course of the next few days, these astronauts would make one of the most fateful journeys of human history. After reaching lunar orbit, they used the lunar module to travel to the surface of the moon. Neil Armstrong was the first to emerge from this module, saying the now famous words as he touched the moon's surface: 'One small step for man, one giant leap for mankind.' After performing many experiments, the astronauts were all able to safely return home. To read more about the Apollo program, look at the panel to your left. To learn more about the Saturn V, look at the panel to your right."

"Melchior told me this story before, or at least something similar, but every time it still gets me. To look up at the moon and know that humans once stood on its surface is an indescribable feeling."

"It is for sure. But somehow, to me, it's also a reminder of how small we are. Even with all this brilliance and cooperation, considering the scale of the universe, we barely even left our home. We exist in such a small, small way if you look through a cosmic lens."

"Dreary as ever, Quinn."

"It's not dreary. It actually makes me feel better that the demise of humanity isn't *that* important."

I give him no other response but an eye-roll. He's just being facetious. Mostly. The two of us continue our stroll down the path and further into the future.

We walk through a world of innovations, but I'm still in awe of the story about the moon landing. I wonder if humanity will ever get to see anything like that again. We arrive at the end of the path, with the year 1998 marking the floor.

"In 1998, one of the most ambitious projects in the history of space exploration was launched: the ISS or International Space Station. The space station was assembled in Earth's orbit, meaning for the first two years of its existence it remained uncrewed. Orbiting 400 kilometers above the surface of the Earth, the ISS would come to house astronauts and cosmonauts from all around the world. These space explorers are constantly experimenting in the unique environment that the ISS provides. In fact, they are almost certainly experimenting right now as you read this! To learn more about the construction of the ISS, read the panel to your right. To learn more about the experiments performed on the ISS, read the panel to your left."

I'm sure we are both thinking the same thing and are equally clueless as to the answer, yet I choose to ask him anyway.

"What do you think happened to those on the ISS when Sin hit?"

"Well, they probably lived longer than most of the people down here."

"I couldn't imagine that, watching humanity fall and being absolutely helpless to stop it."

"I'd bet that's how a lot of people on Earth felt as well."

We stand in silence for a little bit, just taking in the rockets and capsules and other space paraphernalia. In my eyes, this place stands as a monument to what we were, and what we could be again.

Wordlessly, we start wandering back towards the entrance. Our experience here has been wonderful certainly, but all things must end, and Quinn and I must return to our work lest we starve.

We return through the path we walked to get here and watch the figurative years go by. I notice a replica of the moon rover that the Apollo missions used, and for some reason feel drawn to it.

"Come on Quinn, let's see what those astronauts felt when they drove across the moon, we won't get another chance like this."

"Fine, but not for too long."

We both plop down into the seats of the rover. Without looking, I reach out to grab the steering wheel, but my hands meet only air. I guess you don't need a steering wheel on the moon. Quinn makes a small chuckle at my error.

"You would have known it doesn't have a steering wheel if you had read the panel."

"Hey, I can't read as fast as you. That's not my fault, leave me alone," I respond coyishly.

"Or also, if you maybe, I don't know, had eyes."

"Stop bullying meeeee," I cry while slowly leaning into him.

"Really? I'm a bully?" Quinn muses, bringing his face closer to mine.

"Oh yeah, totally."

Our lips are only inches apart at this point. My logical self would keep me from going any further but honestly, fuck it, who cares. His face comes closer. We both close our eyes as his lips are almost on mine.

Clank.

We both burst apart and draw our weapons as fast as we can. Someone, or something is in this building with us.

"The noise came from the lobby, I think, so we should try to go out the back way. The drop down to the lower level doesn't look that high, and from there we can get out through the shattered glass panes," Quinn whispers.

I nod in agreement. We do exactly as he said, quietly sneaking down the path, ensuring that we stay low and keep our footfalls quiet. We reach the end of the path once more and I stow my weapon before hopping onto the ledge on the other side of the railing. From up here, the drop looks pretty damn far. I crouch down on the ledge and turn myself so I'm facing backwards. From here, I lower myself and hang on the ledge with my hands. Quinn has been doing the same, so as we hang, we nonverbally begin a countdown to the drop. We release our hands and plummet to the ground simultaneously. The impact is rough, but we get up quickly and start running. If that was a person we heard earlier, they'd have certainly heard us by now. We sprint through the grassy area outside the museum, eventually making our way back to the road.

"This road should connect back up with I-80 in a little bit, I don't really want to risk it by heading back that way."

"Yeah, I agree."

We aren't going to talk about what happened on the rover, but it was nice, a taste of a world I will probably never get.

Chapter 6 - Quinn

June 23

The mountains and pine trees of Colorado have slowly begun to fade into the unending plains of Nebraska. Over the past few weeks, we have encountered a few travelers, but we always made sure to see them before they saw us, so we never had to risk any interaction. We are effectively out of any reserve food that we had built up before we began our journey, so we must make sure we secure enough food every day to sustain ourselves. So far, we haven't had much trouble as small game like rabbits as well as edible plants have been quite abundant. I have noted a large number of plants that Melchior never taught me about, but I'm not in the mood to try to eat unidentified plants like those.

"Quinn, quit scribbling away, it's time to go."

"I wouldn't have started writing if you weren't so slow packing your stuff."

I shut my journal and store it along with my precious pencil in my bag. I have already packed up everything else, so I swing my backpack over my shoulder and begin trudging away from our campsite. The interstate is only a few minutes' walk away from where we camped, so we should be back on track to continue our journey in a little bit. While food seems to be more abundant here than up in Colorado, the scenery isn't all up to par. When this is all over, if we can, I would like to return to Colorado. We stay silent while we walk, taking in the vast empty plains that surround us.

As we reach the road I comment to Ezra, "I don't like this. I feel so exposed."

"It is what it is. We have to follow this road. We don't know any better way to go."

"I guess, but I'll be happy when we get to a more forested area again."

I really wish we had a car. We could skip all this boring walking shit and cut right to the part where we see if humanity can be saved. But unfortunately, this is not in the cards. Looking down at the fractured road, I doubt a normal vehicle would even be able to drive on this. And that's not even mentioning the fact that we have no way of getting gas.

It's still morning so the heat hasn't begun to set in yet. We will probably walk for about an hour or so more before we stop to look for something to eat. I start mentally going over what food I plan to look for this afternoon when Ezra interrupts me.

"Hey, wait Quinn -- is that smoke coming from over there?"

I turn and look to see a thin pillar of smoke rise towards the heavens from a way down the interstate.

"Let's maybe get off the road for a bit in case they come this way."

We walk perpendicular to the interstate for about ten minutes before we turn and start heading parallel towards it. It should be heading straight, and since we have our compass, I doubt that we will get lost.

"Look, I think that's a greenhouse over there," Ezra exclaims, "If it was sealed up before the Rapture and hasn't been opened since, it's possible that there could be a bunch of untainted food just waiting for us."

I turn my gaze to the northeast of us, maybe about five hundred feet or so, and see what Ezra is talking about.

It's a decently sized greenhouse connected to a decaying farmhouse. Judging by the fencing I see surrounding the area, it seems likely to me that this land used to be used for cattle farming.

"How do we know that someone doesn't live there?"

"Because if someone lived there, they probably wouldn't have a food source like that just sitting out in the open. Plus, it's not like farming exists anymore. If anyone were to open that greenhouse, they are exposing it to Sin, even if they just track in a tiny leaf or piece of grass on their feet, it will jeopardize the entire lot of food."

"True, but we should still be on our guard."

As we walk to the greenhouse, I dart my eyes around the area, double checking to ensure that I don't see any movement. Once we are closer to the house, I can tell that while much of it is rusting, it is holding together better than one would expect a house would after being neglected for so many years. However, we can also clearly see that within the greenhouse, there is a plethora of vegetables growing within it, from peppers to eggplants to squash. My mind begins to plot the various ways I could prepare these vegetables, causing me to lose track of my surroundings. We arrive at the entrance to the greenhouse, standing in front of a decorated glass door separating us from a full supply of food. Ezra goes to open it, but as he turns the handle, he finds it to be locked. At this exact moment, I hear the door to the farmhouse about ten feet behind us swing open. I reach for my weapon holstered at my hip, but before I can even draw it, I hear a gravelly voice come from behind me.

"Drop your weapons you little food thieving shits. On your knees! Now!"

We slowly turn and place our weapons on the ground, as we have no intention of getting shot by the double barrel shotgun that he has trained on us. After, we lower ourselves to our knees and put our hands behind our heads. We see that the man holding the shotgun appears to be fairly old, but still possesses corded muscles from a lifetime of manual labor. He seems like the kind of no-nonsense person who won't tolerate any bullshit.

"Sir, we are very sorry, we did not realize that anyone lived here. We meant you no harm and would appreciate it if you would kindly let us leave," Ezra says in a slow, rhythmic manner.

"Oh, and have you come back and kill me tonight? I don't think so."

"Sir, I understand your apprehension. It is a dangerous world we live in, but we were simply passing by the area and thought that this greenhouse was a pre-Rapture relic. If you let us, we will be on our way."

"If you're just a traveler as you say, what brings you to these parts? Where are you going?"

"We are heading to South Bend, Indiana from Northern Colorado. As for why, well that's harder to answer. The short of it is that we believe a cure for Sin is being made in South Bend. I know you probably don't believe us, but if you will allow me to reach into my backpack, I can show you proof."

He gestures with his weapon before saying, "Do it, but don't try anything funny or you're going to lose that pretty face of yours."

Ezra reaches into his bag, digging for the email that we found at the Ichthys facility. After a few seconds of searching, I see that the man is getting a little anxious that Ezra might be searching for a weapon of some type.

"Got it," he mouths under his breath.

Slowly, he extracts the letter from the bag, careful not to give the man any more of a reason to shoot him. I can see the man tighten his finger around the trigger as Ezra's hand exits the bag. Once he sees that it really is only a letter, it loosens again. My heart is beating incredibly rapidly, but I keep myself focused on the moment, observing every detail, every escape route, every sway of my opponent so that if the time comes, I will have the advantage. Ezra tosses the letter in front of the man. He kneels to collect it while keeping his weapon concentrated on Ezra and me.

He unfolds the letter and starts to read through its message. Now is the moment of truth: if he is unwilling to accept what's on that paper, Ezra and I are going to be in an immense amount of trouble. I see his facial expression begin to shift slowly as he makes his way through the letter. It seems like quite an unbelievable story, and one doesn't survive in this world by being overly trusting. However, if he doesn't believe us, how do we proceed from here? Is he going to execute us for the crime of coming near his garden? If it came to that, I would charge him and try to get in front of the weapon so it would only hit me and give Ezra a chance to escape.

"Well shit," the man says, tossing the paper back to Ezra, "And you say that this first branch is in South Bend?"

"Yes, sir, it is," Ezra replies.

"I must say, if this is some ploy to try and trick me you certainly have jumped the shark… but I don't think it is. Unless you are one of the best actors I have ever seen, have access to a machine that could produce this letter and have one hell of an imagination, what you're saying must be true. I am sorry for this misunderstanding, but as I'm sure you are aware, one can never be too cautious in this world. I have some food and drink if you would be willing to accept it as my apology."

As we both start to stand up, I interject, "No, thank you, we really-"

"Yes, please we would like that very much," Ezra interrupts, giving me a light jab to my side.

"I will ask that you surrender your weapons to me before we enter. That letter just showed me you aren't a pair of marauding raiders, not that you aren't necessarily dangerous. And don't worry, you will get them back when you leave."

I begrudgingly comply and Ezra appears to do the same. I don't like this at all, but given that free food is on the line, I'm willing to make some compromises. Plus, this man already has us completely at his mercy. If he wanted us dead, we would be dead. We take all the weapons out of our bag and place them at his feet. The man opens the door to the farmhouse and gestures us in.

We enter to see a surprisingly clean kitchen and dining room area. There is a four-person table at the center of this room, which is surrounded by different cabinets and kitchen appliances lining the walls of the room. Over the sink and stove are some large windows looking out upon the endless plains engulfing this little bastion of human existence. There are two doors that connect this room to other parts of the house. One of them is open and seems to lead to a family room of sorts, while the other is closed.

"Take a seat. By the way, my name's Doug, in case you were wondering."

"I'm Ezra."

"I'm Quinn."

"Nice to meet you two. It's not often I get any friendly company out here."

"It's a lonely world," I reply.

"That it is. I have something special for you two that you probably haven't had in quite a long time, if ever."

I don't know what he's talking about, but it immediately sets me on edge. Maybe this is a mistake. If something does go wrong, I'm sure I can-

"Pancakes!" Doug exclaims, interrupting me mid-thought.

"Pancakes?" Ezra questions.

"You do know what pancakes are right?"

"No, I do, but how could you possibly make them?"

"Well before the Rapture I was what a lot of people called a prepper, meaning that I stocked up on a bunch of goods in preparation for the apocalypse. One of those goods was pancake mix. It hasn't been opened since before the rapture so it's Sin-free. Oh, and don't worry, it doesn't go bad."

"Oh, wow, that sounds amazing. Thank you so much!"

"The least I can do after causing you both so much trouble earlier. I'm going to get the mix; I'll be back in a few minutes."

"Okay."

This was certainly different than what I expected. Doug seems to have… a kindness, one you don't find in the wasteland very often. By this point, I'm almost certain that we are safe here; logically and emotionally I can't see what reason Doug has for harming us. If Ezra and I ever do cure Sin, I would want to come back here and help him out.

"Quinn, this is so exciting! We never had pre-Rapture food before."

"Well technically that isn't true. You did eat that can of Spam that one time a few years back."

"Don't make me think of that please. That was, erm... not a highlight of my experience on this planet of ours."

"I had some too. It's not like you suffered alone."

"Even more reason for you to not want to bring it up!"

We hear footsteps approaching the door, so we decide that it's probably better to avoid discussing gastronomic catastrophes of the past. Doug opens the door and emerges carrying a box of Aunt Jemima's pancake mix.

"Hey, just out of curiosity, why don't you keep the pancake mix in the kitchen?"

"Well, it's really only for special occasions. I like to keep my food stores down in the basement in a special container so I can try to ensure Sin doesn't get in em."

We nod our heads in understanding. It's weird to think that this is the first time I've spoken to someone other than Ezra in probably about a month. The last person was Ja-... no I don't want to think about that.

"Woah, is that a working electric stove?"

I turn my eyes to what Ezra is referring to and am met by the surprising sight of a functioning electric appliance.

"Yeah, it is. You couldn't see it from the front, but I actually have some solar panels on the other side of the farmhouse roof."

"Working electricity, pancakes, you really are living the life here aren't you?"

As he begins pouring the now-liquidy pancake mix onto the pan, he replies, "In many ways I am. I suppose what "the life" is has certainly changed in the past 15 years."

Doug was a very imposing man. Seeing him wear a cute apron and cooking broke the veil of ultra-masculinity I had subconsciously placed upon him. I have no idea why I saw him this way, but I guess having your first encounter with someone occur at the barrel end of a shotgun could do that.

"Could I get you something to drink while the pancakes cook?"

"Yes, just some water please," Ezra responds.

"Some water for me as well, thank you."

He opens a refrigerator and takes out a tall glass bottle of water. The condensation on it gives it that opaque look, which makes me even more thirsty. He pours the water into two glasses that he got out of the cabinets and passes them to us. Both Quinn and I begin to chug like maniacs.

"Woah there, I would have got that for you sooner if I knew you were that thirsty!"

"Oh, no, there's no reason to worry about it."

"As much as I enjoy our conversation, I need some time to just focus on the pancakes. After all, I am cooking for company."

We sit in the homey kitchen, about to share a meal cooked on an actual electric stove. It's something that I didn't think I would ever get to experience. They say you only know you were happy once you have lost it. Well, I think I can say I'm happy now because I know that I'm going to lose it. Once Ezra and I leave here, it's back to the harsh life we endure on the road. But for now, in this moment, we have something special, an experience of a world that truly has been lost to time.

"Okay you two, I got your pancakes coming right up!"

"Thank you!" we both respond.

He takes out two plates from a drawer in the kitchen and uses his spatula to flip the pancakes out of the pan and onto the plates. It looks like he made five medium sized pancakes, setting aside two for each of us and one for himself.

As he walks over to us, plates in hand he says, "I'm sorry that I couldn't add any maple syrup, but unfortunately I ran out of that a long time ago."

"Don't worry, this is the best meal we will have had in years!" Ezra responds.

"Glad I could help," he says while sliding the plates in front of us.

Quinn and I both begin to dig in, cutting the pancakes as fast as we can and shoving it down our months. It is heavenly. I see a smile burst across Doug's face as he slowly chips away at his pancake.

"Now that breakfast is served, I have some questions for you."

"Ask away." I reply.

"So that letter you showed me, how did you come to find it? I mean stumbling into the base of some weird international organization that controlled the response to Sin sounds pretty crazy."

"The story doesn't get any less crazy. The village Quinn and I were staying in got attacked by another group. We stole one of their cars to try to get away, but eventually we got forced off the road. We fell down a ditch and they just assumed that was the end of it. But really, we were in an underground parking lot for this Ichthys facility. We searched through it and found that email right there," I respond.

"To me, based on that email it seems like Sin must have been bio-weapon or something along those lines. The email said that it comes from the "Egg." That's got to be an emission system for it. I could never decide whether I thought Sin was man-made or divine retribution, but I mean what you just showed me has it pretty clear," Doug states, clearly very interested in the subject.

"In my eyes Sin doesn't make sense as a bio-weapon. There is no way to use it in isolation. If one country tried to target another with Sin and released it, it would end up coming back to destroy the original country. But Ichthys said they were responsible, so they must have had some role in releasing it. But who would ever develop it and why? I just don't understand."

"Yeah, it could have been some type of bio-weapon. If it was, they didn't want to release it though," Ezra replies in between bites.

"I'm sorry about your village though. It's a cruel world after all, but know that I understand your pain. How did you two come to meet? Was it in that village?" Doug asked.

"No, before the Rapture we both lived on the same floor of an apartment building in Bakersfield, California. Sin got our parents, so when everyone on the floor decided to leave town, they sort of took us in along with some other orphaned kids. One of the people who lived there taught us and a few of the other kids everything we know about living in the wasteland. He was everything to us, and I know for certain that Ezra and I wouldn't be alive without him. But... he's gone now and so is the group. Quinn and I ended up staying together, and we have been wandering alone for a few years now." Ezra explained.

"It's good that you two managed to stick together. Being able to have someone to rely on like you guys do is so important - I hope you realize that. Make sure you never let each other go."

Letting Ezra go is an idea that doesn't even seem like a choice. It's on the same level of possibility as learning to fly or time travel. As long as I live, I will always be there for him and vice versa. That is the pact we made.

Doug pauses his questioning to allow us to finish gobbling down our breakfast. These pancakes are so delicious that it is almost indescribable. It doesn't even seem real that people in the old times had food like this multiple times a day. They were so lucky.

As Ezra chews the last bite of his food he says, "Wow, that was amazing. We are forever in your debt."

"It's really the least I can do, I promise. You know, I really like you two. You both are real and genuine in a way I'm not used to. And, well, let's just say it gets a little lonely out here. I'm sure you two must be tired from your long trip. I could offer you an actual bed to sleep in for a few days."

"A bed?"

"Yep."

I don't think I've slept in an actual, not moldy and falling apart, but warm and comfortable bed in a very, very long time. I think that the last time may have been when I was only seven or eight years old. While I am incredibly eager to get back to our journey, and I'm sure Ezra is too, this opportunity is simply far too tantalizing to pass up.

"You can't just offer us something as amazing as that and expect us to be able to refuse." Ezra tells him gleefully.

"I'm simply glad to share what I have with someone who I suspect deserves it."

If it wasn't for what happened earlier, I would be highly suspicious of this offer. However, I keep coming back to the idea that if he wanted us dead or unconscious, it would already have happened. I don't understand why he's been so willing to trust us. He may have proven himself to us, but other than through our words, we have not proven ourselves to him.

"I know it's morning, but I might as well show you where the bedrooms are, come on."

We stand up from the dinner table and start following Doug. He leads us through the open door, and we enter a nice family room area with a couch, some chairs, and a TV!

"Wait, is that - a television?" I burst with excitement.

"Hehe, it is. I don't keep it plugged in most of the time because the solar grid can only run the stove or the TV at any one time. And it's not like there are any broadcasts anymore. For all intents and purposes, it's just a hunk of electronics. Although, it does have a DVD player and I do have some movies on DVD, so if you ever want to watch some during your stay at Chateau Doug, just let me know and I can get that going for you."

"Wow, thank you so much, I can't believe it," I tell him excitedly.

"You should. Sometimes good things just happen to good people."

I'd like to believe that, but from my experience terrible things happen to all kinds of people. Exhibit A: the Rapture. Exhibit B: The murder of all the people in my first tribe. Exhibit C: The murder of all the people in our village. The world is cruel and will continue to be cruel, but I suppose that just means I should take this repose when I can get it.

"You two can explore the house after, but for now come on let me show you where you are staying. Once we get up there you can drop off those giant bags of yours."

We nod and follow him up the stairs. They creak and groan as we walk but show no indication that they might give in any time soon. The stairs lead out into a long hallway with multiple doors. He opens the second one on the right and gestures for us to enter.

"This room used to belong to my... uhh... never mind. It has a pretty good view out onto what used to be the cattle fields, so there's that. It only has one bed, but I'm sure you two are no strangers to being close to each other if you have lived with him for your entire life."

"This is wonderful, really I can't thank you enough."

"It's really my pleasure. After you two get settled, feel free to explore downstairs, just don't break anything or go down into the basement."

I look around the room and see that it's plain save for a few old baseball trophies sitting upon a shelf. It triggers something in my mind, and I instantly understand why Doug was so willing to let us stay here. I suppose we both get something out of this then. Ezra leaps into the bed and just lies there.

"Oh my god, Quinn this is amazing you have to try it."

"Alright, if you say so!"

I jump on to the bed, but from the other direction that Ezra did. He yelps in surprise as I body slam down onto him.

"Hey!! That hurts," he says as he makes an overly exaggerated frowny face.

"Poor baby."

I shift myself off his body and lay parallel next to him. I allow myself to sink deep into the mattress. This is so, so, so very nice. Why couldn't I have been born just a little bit earlier so I could enjoy the fruits of modern life, just for a little bit? But thanks to Doug, I'm going to at least get a taste of what it was like.

As we lay in bed, Ezra turns to me and says, "You know Quinn, I think we are going to have a great time here."

Interlude - Phantasmagoria

Down

Down

Down

Down

Down

The room is black and cold. The winds of Helheim seep through my skin, into my blood, through my bones and beyond. The water around my ankles begins to gradually creep up my atrophied legs. No, not water, but blood. Blood like wine, blood I have indulged in during my time above. Ichor oozes from the ceiling, from the walls, and out the mouth of the rotting carcass crucified before me. No, no, no, no, I didn't. That wasn't me. I didn't bring you down here that was... his name is gone.

Two holes in his chest. Was that me? The sanguine sea has risen so that I am floating, with the roof quickly approaching. Am I doomed to drown in this stony sepulcher? My face is pressed against the granite above me. No, not granite, but bone. Bones I have laid bare during my time above. I shut my eyes and wait for the blood to come pouring down my throat, but it does not.

I float in an empty white void, if I could be considered an "I," that is. A body I have not and not what you would traditionally call a mind either. What am I? Why am I? How did I get here? I try to scream, but I have no throat to use. I try to jump, but I have no legs to command. I try to wave, but I have no arms to direct. There he stands, right in front of me, but I cannot reach him. Why can't I reach him? I move towards him, but when I get to him, he is gone. And so am I.

I stand on the cliff, overlooking an endless ocean of fluid grass. The figure below me warbles sounds of different pitches and tones, but the message is clear: I need to jump. I don't want to jump, but for some reason I trust the figure below. I take a running start and prepare to leap, but at the last second just before my legs leave the ground I hesitate. Behind me I hear a stomping noise, and as I turn, I see why I needed to jump. The spike of black rock at the tip of the demon's arm impales me through the chest. I stare into its shifting and jagged head as he flings me off the cliff, blood pouring out of the hole where my heart used to be. I fall

Down
Down
Down
Down
Down

Chapter 7 - Ezra

June 25

I awake to the sound of Quinn's screams, something I wish to never hear again. I immediately enter high alert mode, first looking for a threat before I even check on Quinn. Seeing nothing other than an empty room, my focus shifts to Quinn himself. He is sitting up in bed and sweating profusely.

"Quinn are you alright?" I soothe as I place my hand on his shoulder.

"Yeah, I'm alright, don't worry. It was just a bad dream."

"Do you want to talk about it?"

"No, not really. I'm not even sure how I would explain it even if I wanted to."

"That's okay, I understand what you mean."

"Do you think you could-" he pauses for a second, considering what he is going to say next, "Do you think you could come here for a bit?"

I roll over on the bed and nestle myself, so he is spooning me. I feel his strong arms clasp around me very tightly. Whatever his dream was about must have shaken him deeply, but I am by no means complaining. His firm embrace completes me in a way that nothing else can. The past two days have been such a fantasy, living here in this house, enjoying the comforts of modern technology and settled living. This just completes all of it. It's so easy to imagine that we are just lying in bed at our house, just waiting to get up and go to work in a minute. I suppose the world we inhabit makes it very easy to find escape in our own heads. I wonder if it was that way for the people that lived before the Rapture too.

The door to our room suddenly swings open. Quinn and I scramble apart from each other, but as I turn to face Doug, I can see that the damage has been done. The look on his face is an indescribable mixture of surprise and embarrassment, coupled with a hint of disgust.

"I just heard what sounded like a scream come from up here, but I mean clearly I misinterpreted." The anger slowly rises in his voice as he speaks.

"No, Doug, it's not what it looks like. Quinn just had a nightmare, and I was comforting him."

"'Comforting' huh? Is that what they call it these days?"

"That's not it at all, I promise, this is just a misunderstanding."

"I let you two into my *home*. I let you stay here like family, and this is what you do! In my *son's room* of all places!"

I quickly become worried that this encounter could become violent, but I am still going to try to do everything that I possibly can to prevent that from happening. Doug is a good man, he's just a bit unstable now.

"Doug, we promise we did not mean any harm to you or the sanctity of your home. We will leave immediately if that is what you want-"

"Oh, so you are admitting it now. Does that mean you lied to me earlier?"

Quinn, who usually stays silent in most social encounters, stands and walks up to Doug.

"Sir, we didn't do anything wrong. We apologize t-"

Doug slaps Quinn across the face with the back of his hand. In response, Quinn clenches his fists and stares directly into Doug's eyes. I truly expect him to take a swing at Doug, so I leap out of bed in preparation to assist him.

"We thank you for the hospitality you have shown. We will be leaving in just a moment after we put our clothes on."

He shuts the door in Doug's face, walks over and grabs his bag and pulls out his jeans and a t-shirt, then calls to me saying, "Come on Ezra, we're leaving."

I quickly throw on my clothes and swing my bag over my shoulder. After tidying up the room and making our final preparations, we open the door to the bedroom and start to walk out. Doug stands speechless in the hall. He already has an air of regret starting to cloud around him. He did not want to take this as far as he ended up taking it. Quinn lightly pushes him out of the doorway and the pair of us trudge down the hallway towards the stairs. This truly is such a shameful end to such a nice time.

"Wait, no, I'm sorry I - I didn't mean to get physical, that was a -"

"Enjoy your life, Doug, we hold nothing against you," Quinn says, maintaining an unemotional tone of voice.

While I am very pleased that it seems like an uncomfortable situation is going to end without any bloodshed, I'm utterly shocked at how Quinn is acting here. Not to say that he isn't mature, but it's rare that he takes the lead in circumstances like these, and even more rare that he is so willing to absolve the offending party of any wrongdoing. But if this is what Quinn wants to do, I will follow him. Yesterday, Doug told us that our weapons were in the coat closet by the door in case we wanted to go hunting. Good thing, I wouldn't see him telling us in this state.

We walk down the stairs, through the kitchen, grab our weapons, and head out the door we walked in two days ago. The morning is misty and humid, but we have slept later than we normally would in the comfort of that warm bed, so it is at least light out. We walk for a while back to I-80 before I consider trying to talk to him about what had just happened. It all happened so fast that I'm still trying to process it. Even though Doug thought we were doing something we obviously were not, it still kind of shocks me that he could have such a reaction. I know that people like me had some troubles before the Rapture, but I mean, we are all just struggling to survive here. I feel like no one should give a shit about who someone else likes when any day we could turn into goop from eating the wrong thing.

"Quinn, are you okay? I know that was a lot, but you handled it really well."

"Yeah, I'm fine. I'm actually a little surprised too. When he slapped me, something came over me, like a desire to show that I'm better than he was and not give into emotion like he did. And I do think Doug is a good man, just a little caught up in the past. But then again, who wouldn't be when the present is like this?"

"It all just feels so sudden."

"I would imagine that's how people felt during the Rapture but amplified a few thousand times."

The road ahead of me consumes my eyes. Back again to the dull, cracked, empty, and depressing road. I almost wish I had never seen that greenhouse or met Doug. It feels so sour after everything that happened, but I know that I still enjoyed it in the moment. But at this bitter end, the memories of such a good time give me not pleasure in their existence, but pain in their loss.

"I think the crux of the problem is change. We, and people in general, hate drastic and unwanted change like the one we just experienced. Both a change in our relationship with Doug and a change in our living conditions. And it feels not like change, but like loss," I hypothesize to Quinn, eager to start a discussion to get our minds away from what just happened.

"Well, isn't loss just a part of change?"

"What do you mean?"

"Change means the erasure of one thing followed by its replacement with another thing. What we consider to be 'loss' is change without that second part of replacement. But that means that even when there is a net gain from change, it still feels like 'loss' to some extent because it is."

"I mean I guess that makes sense, Professor Ezra."

"I'm just trying to come up with a good answer."

"I think the more obvious answer is just that we hate change - when what we get is worse than what we had. For example, I don't know, maybe going from a nice comfortable house to a shitty sleeping bag?" he suggests, adding just a bit of levity to the conversation.

"I think you are forgetting that the shitty sleeping bag also comes with the possibility of finding a cure to Sin."

"Trust me, I am *not* forgetting that. Otherwise, we would be trying to find some place to settle down."

When he brings up settling down my mind flickers to the village. When Quinn and I used to walk through it to offer trading goods with the people that settled there, I always loved to see the bustle of all the different people. Children, old people, young adults, all dead or scattered now. That's the danger of settled life.

"Hopefully, when we make it to South Bend, they will have a bed we can rest in."

"Oddly enough, the idea of a bed sounds about just as good as a cure for Sin."

"I think you'll be singing a different tune once you find a batch of delicious mushrooms or whatever you look for and can't eat because they have Sin."

"That's probably true, but it's also a problem for future me to deal with, so I will be content in my desire for a bed right now."

The gray fog covers the road up ahead and we only can see for a bit in front of us, so Quinn and I have to be on our guard even more than we usually would in case someone comes up on us. It's going to be a long day.

*   *   *

While the sleeping bag certainly does feel good after a long day of travel and hunting, it certainly is no bed. The moon hangs over us in the cloudless night sky, adding in some beauty to an otherwise barren day. The last embers of the fire between Quinn and I glow a dull red as they cool off, making me even more tired as the light fades. The moon above regains my attention.

"The moon is absolutely so weird. Like it's just a big hunk of rock that floats above the earth. It's literally so massive that we can't even comprehend how large it is. All the distance we have traveled in our lifetime would only add up to a fraction of the circumference of it. I feel like we just see it so often that we lose perspective on how strange it is."

"I wouldn't really say that that makes it weird. The moon is the way it is and always has been that way."

"I disagree. Something is weird when it is different from what is traditional. Thinking about the moon in the way of a floating space rock that acts as a huge mirror for the sun's light is a different way of thinking about the moon compared to what is traditionally thought, making it weird."

"Anything can be 'weird' if you describe it in that way, but everything isn't weird, is it?"

"No, it's just the moon seems so fantastical, something that you would find in some strange fantasy book, not in our actual sky."

"Okay then Ezra, I will let you enjoy your lunar musings."

I stare at the moon for a few moments more, taking in the various craters and shadows that I can see from hundreds of thousands of miles away. I wonder if Earth will lose its name to the people that live in the future. Sin will continue to spread, but maybe someone somewhere will find a cure of some sort, protecting just a small fraction of the population, creating a bottleneck of humans unlike anything seen before. Maybe those people would call our little blue marble something totally different. And if these hypothetical people do come to exist, they almost have something of a gift. A chance of rebuilding humanity to be better than what it was before. I know that a clean slate is something that many people that lived before the Rapture would clamor for. I know that I would too.

My thoughts drift back to the tumultuous events of this morning. In that moment lying in his arms, I felt such peace. I just want to have that forever. Is that really too much to ask? But saying it, asking him, forcing the words out of my throat just seems like something truly impossible. How could I possibly ask to change things after we have been like this for so long. It makes me want to scream. To have him so close but be unable to have him. It just tears at-

Crunch.

Someone's nearby. They don't seem to have any sort of light on considering that I don't see any glow coming from around me, but that crunching sound is distinctly the noise of footfalls on sticks. The fire is completely out now, and we have no standing structures that would indicate we are camping here. I'm sure that Quinn is awake and aware as much as I am. We both know that any sort of fight in the dark here would pose a huge risk since we are at such an information deficit right now. Who the fuck is just wandering around with no lights in the middle of wilderness? This whole situation is just so thoroughly confusing to me.

My heart is beating incredibly fast, and a sweat is beginning to develop across my brow. What a world we have where any indication of human life makes me think that a deadly encounter is on the horizon. The crunching sound continues to get louder as they approach the camp. I can sound out now that it's two people. They seem to be coming from the left of me, so considering that Quinn lies to the right of me, they would notice me before him. My worries grow with each footfall. My revolver is sitting in my bag just behind my sleeping bag. It would probably take about five seconds to get it out of the back and draw it, so if they notice me while I'm lying here it will already be too late. The worst part of this is that I can't even try to coordinate with Quinn.

I resolve to myself that if they approach within my best approximation of 10 feet, I will draw my weapon on them. I imagine that Quinn would do the same since he is probably waiting on my signal. It really would be much better if we could all walk away from this situation unharmed, but unfortunately if we want to ensure our survival, Quinn and I can't take the most peaceful approach. I count mentally how much time I have until I need to draw my weapon. Five. Four. Three. Two. On-

"We've been walking around here for hours, and we still can't find them, let's just head back." The voice of a woman softly calls to her companion.

"Based on what we found last time, we are definitely getting closer. We shouldn't just go back now," a different female voice responds to the first with a slightly peeved tone.

"That doesn't mean that we should just stumble around in the dark for hours. We have to do this right."

"But-"

"Let's go, we can get up early and set out as dawn breaks."

I'm still prepared to leap out of my bag and grab my weapon, but I can hear that they are starting to move in the opposite direction. What were they talking about? I think one of them said they wanted to "find *them*". Does that mean us? Why would anyone want to find us? And even if someone did, how would they track us across hundreds of miles of American highway? Unless Doug sent someone to find us to apologize. No, that wouldn't make sense. Doug doesn't have any family. If they are searching for us, I doubt that they have friendly intentions. They don't have any idea that we're here, so maybe I should try a preemptive strike. For a moment, I deeply consider grabbing my weapon and shooting the pair of them. Then I realize that since it's so dark and they have gotten farther away, there's a good chance that I will miss my shot. I have no desire to get into a gunfight in the middle of night with an unknown enemy.

Damn it. I should have taken my shot when I had the chance. I know that I could be wrong about this whole situation, but the truth is that it's a kill or be killed world. If I want to protect Quinn and myself, I must make these kinds of tough decisions. Now, because of my inaction, Quinn and I have this unknown threat that is going to loom over us for the rest of the journey. From now on we should probably set up a system of watches to make sure those two can't ambush us in the night. Tonight, we got lucky, but I have no desire to rely on luck in the future. I decide to wait about ten minutes to make sure that they are really gone before I go and approach Quinn. Over the course of those ten minutes, I stew in my own failure and try to prevent self-destructive thoughts from consuming me. After my approximation of ten minutes has ended, I crawl out of my sleeping bag and walk over to Quinn.

As I approach, he sits up in his sleeping bag and says, "What the fuck was that?"

"It was two women, and they were looking for someone. I have no idea why they would be, but I have a sinking feeling that it might be us. We are going to have to be more careful from now on."

"This doesn't make any sense, are you sure that you heard them, right?"

"I mean they could be looking for someone totally different that's in this area, but that just seems to be too much of a coincidence for me to be able to excuse. And one more thing, they said that they would be up early in the morning to keep looking, so we probably shouldn't stay here."

"Ughhh," he groans. "This sucks. And to think we were sleeping soundly in a nice, safe house less than a day ago."

"I'm sorry, really, this is my fault. I should have taken them out once I realized what they were doing."

"What? No, Ezra, you can't just kill them for the crime of wandering about in the forest. And don't give me any bullshit about 'needing to protect me and yourself.' If we do that, we're just as bad as the raiders."

Why did I bring this up with him? I knew this is how he would respond. *Get it together, Ezra.*

"We can talk about this later. We have to leave now if we want to get some semblance of a night's rest."

"Fine," he says, although he is clearly not done with this topic.

We pack up our sleeping bags and make our way back to the interstate. We don't want to attract any unwanted attention, so we try to utilize the light of the full moon to be able to navigate. Quickly, we make it to the road and start to follow it. Quinn and I are both too cranky to have any pleasant conversation, so we walk in silence through the night. At least it's not as hot now as it is during the day, but that doesn't make up for the crushing drowsiness dominating my mind. I'm so tired that I honestly wouldn't be too opposed to just collapsing in the grass on the side of the road. But then I think back to our potential pursuers, and I find the strength once more to continue walking.

While thinking about the ones chasing us, I realize that in a strange turn of fate, it might have been better that we left Doug's this morning. If those women went the same way we did, there's a chance that they might have stopped by Doug's house too. I do still hope that they missed his house as I don't want Doug to be put in any danger even after all that has happened, but it is good that Quinn and I never had to face the possibility of a shootout there. I can't rationalize why anyone would be looking for us. I mean, there was that man that had to shoot back in the village, but all those raiders probably think we are dead after we crashed. Maybe they are Ichthys agents sent to find us after we discovered one of their branches. Oh, how wonderful that would be, to have some knights in shining armor come save us and bring us straight to a nice, secure location where we can stay indefinitely. I recede from the mental river I had been swimming through and return my focus to what's in front of me: the road, the moon, and Quinn, some of the only constants in my life.

Chapter 8 - Quinn

July 13

I turn and look back over my shoulder to see the decaying skyscrapers of Omaha. Vines grow across the ones still standing, giving the effect that they are pillars of plant life greater than any tree on the planet. Some of them have fallen over from disrepair. I think, how fast we can lose something that took thousands of years to build. I could never imagine living in one of those towers back when they stood as a monolith to humanity's greatness rather than its folly. I feel like I would be in constant fear that it would just collapse at any moment. I suppose they are probably just as safe as any home would be, but hey, monkey brain will do what monkey brain does.

"I wonder if there are any people living there," Ezra asks me, turning and walking backwards as he does.

"Probably, but if there are, I doubt they're friendly."

"Yeah, the city would provide some good shelter, but I doubt there's much food in there, so they probably wouldn't be too friendly to outsiders."

"You know I still find it crazy that people used to live so close to each other like that. Like if you lived in an apartment, you would have thousands of people within a mile of you at any given time. I don't even think I remember seeing more than a tenth of that many people in my whole life."

"There were a lot more people back then," he says with a hint of sadness in his voice.

We let his words hang in the air for a while, taking in their significance. I often think about how many people are left. A billion? 500 million? 100? Fewer? And worst of all is that I will never get an answer, but nonetheless the question clings to me. I decide to break the silence to try to get my mind off the enormity of the loss our species has suffered.

"I wonder what that city will look like in ten years. Maybe someday you would never even know that it was there."

"Maybe, but I hope not. There's something sad in being forgotten. It's like that saying, 'You die twice, once when you stop breathing and again the last time your name is spoken.'"

"But there is also something redeeming in forgetting. All the sins we made, wiped away, destroyed in a way that nothing but true erasure can. By your quote, both a life and a tragedy can only be truly wiped away in forgetting."

"I suppose, but does that really mea-"

The force of the impact throws Ezra forward and to the ground before I even hear the gunshot. Blood comes pouring out of his left shoulder, spilling out onto the blistering pavement. It takes me a moment to realize what has happened, but once I do, I don't even think before I react, scooping up Ezra with both of my arms princess style. I've heard people say that in stressful situations like this, adrenaline gives you strength that you never knew you had. They were right. He barely even feels like a weight as I sprint towards the tall grass on the other side of the street. I run in a slightly zig-zag pattern to try to prevent my attacker from being able to hit me too. I feel a bullet whizz by my head and slam into a tree that sprouted in the middle of the road up ahead.

I hop over the railing on the side of the road and continue sprinting through the tall grass. Judging from the way Ezra fell, the shot came from behind. That means they shouldn't be able to see me well in this grass. Before I entered, I took note of an old barn a few hundred yards away, but it's also well behind me; I doubt the shooter would expect me to head in their direction - making it the perfect spot to hide. I can't see exactly where I'm going in the grass, but I angle myself so that I'm heading in the approximate direction that I saw the barn.

No thoughts are passing through my mind. I remain wholly focused on the task ahead of me. The blood from Ezra's wound is pouring on to my black shirt, staining the cloth as well as my mind. I know in that moment I will never forget what I see looking down upon his blood-soaked body. He looks up at me and grimaces, which at least lets me know that he's still conscious. I pant heavily, as I burst through the other side of the field of tall grass. The barn is less than one hundred feet away. I don't see any signs of the shooter as I make my sprint across the open field under the late afternoon sun. I reach the barn and make my way around to its far side. The main gate is closed, but I see a small door next to it. I run up to it and lower Ezra next to it. He's still awake, but I can tell that he's in a lot of pain. All the more reason I can't make any mistakes right now. I try to open the door, but it won't budge. I look at Ezra as I place him down and see that he is trying to say something to me, but I'm too focused on trying to get us to safety to pause and talk to him. I raise my foot and kick the handle, which buckles, but doesn't break. I raise my foot and try again focusing all my energy, all my will, all my pent-up rage to break this small little metal lock separating us from safety. My foot lands heavily against the door but still, it refuses to break. The force of my kick knocks me back and I land on my ass, staring at Ezra's bleeding body and the rickety wooden door standing in my way.

I stand up and prepare for one final attempt. This time, I elect to body slam the door rather than try to kick it in. I sprint with everything I have towards the door. I'm so overrun by emotion I almost let out a war cry of sorts before remembering I need to keep my position secret. As I slam my body against the door, I almost think that it will push me back one more time, but finally, I hear the metal latch snap, causing me to crash to the floor, inside the barn. I stand with no injuries but a bruised ego and run over to Ezra, picking him up slowly this time to avoid injuring him further. I take him inside the barn and shut the door behind us, although I am unable to lock it. Next to some hay bales to the left of the barn I see a trapdoor that presumably leads to a cellar.

I reach it, place Ezra down, and pull on the circular handle. Luckily, this one is not locked and with some effort, I heave the wooden slab up, revealing concrete steps leading into total darkness. I reach into my bag and pull out my small electric light and place it in my shirt's front pocket. I pick up Ezra and descend into the cellar, careful with my steps knowing this time Ezra won't be there to catch me if I fall. The temperature drops significantly as I walk down, but it is welcome in the summer heat. I reach the bottom to find dirty concrete floors and what appears to be a small room. I prop Ezra against one of the walls and collapse on the cool concrete floor. I'm heaving from the effort exerted during my sprint and just trying to get enough oxygen in me to let me keep helping Ezra. Once my head stops spinning, I head right back up the stairs in order to secure the basement against our attackers.

As I leave, he quietly whispers, "Don't go."

I turn back to face him and put my hand on his unharmed shoulder, "I'll be right back, I'm just closing the door."

He nods as I turn and head back up the stairs, leaving the light with him. Once I make it back up to the barn, I pull a few of the hay bales off the stack and place them in front of the cellar entrance to try to obscure it from the attacker in case they come around this way. After the entrance is appropriately hidden, I close the hatch and slowly return down to Ezra, feeling the walls as I go to make up for my lack of light. Upon reaching him, I bring the light closer to the wound and begin inspecting it. Judging by the blood flow, I don't think it hit any major arteries.

"Can you still move the arm?"

"I think so," he groans.

Then luckily it is probably just a flesh wound. I stand over Ezra so I can access the bag on his back. I rummage through it and find the first aid kit that we had stored. It has some bandages and alcohol in it, but not much else. Shit. This wound is going to need stitches and I don't have any. Not to mention antibiotic cream. Still, I have to do what I can now. I first take out the alcohol and prepare to pour it over the wound to clean it.

"This is going to hurt, okay?"

"Gimme a countdown."

"One, two-"

I pour it on two and he yelps in pain. As much as I hate doing this, it's absolutely necessary. Next, I move on to applying the bandages, careful to make sure I don't get any dirt from the surrounding environment onto them. I feel around the back of his shoulder and notice an exit wound. At least I won't need to dig the bullet out. I use up a large portion of the bandages we have in this kit to make sure that there is enough there to help the blood clot. I'm going to need more if I want to make sure this wound stays clean. By the time I'm done I'm already mentally moving on to the next steps. I need to make sure the wound doesn't get infected, so maybe I should try to cauterize it somehow? No, I can't start a fire in here and if I do one outside it might alert whoever the shooter is. That leaves only one option: I need to go into Omaha. I'm sure there are plenty of hospitals around there and considering how fast Sin hit, I'm sure that there are left over medical supplies just waiting there. Damn it. I really don't want to leave Ezra alone here, but I just don't have any other choice.

"Ezra, I have to go find a sewing kit and some antibiotics, so I'm going to have to leave you here for a little bit."

"No, Quinn. Please don't leave, I don't want to be alone," he begs, making no effort to obscure his desperation.

"Trust me, I wouldn't leave unless it was absolutely necessary. We *cannot* let that wound get infected, so this is just the only way. While I'm gone, I need you to keep as much pressure as you can on that wound to try and prevent the bleeding."

I take out all the vegetables and berries that I had collected during the day and place them in Ezra's lap. He caught a rabbit this morning but unfortunately, we have no way of cooking it.

"I don't know how long I will be gone but you are going to need to eat some of this while I am. Don't save any for me, you can have it all."

I swing my bag over my shoulder and put my handgun in my back pocket.

"Quinn, no. Please don't leave, I - I can't do this alone."

We both know the stakes here. If I don't come back, he won't have the strength to open the cellar door with just one arm. This basement would become his tomb. I will not allow that to happen, no matter the cost.

"I love you, Ezra," I say as I exit his view.

I heave open the trap door and walk out into the barn. I close the door behind me and place a hay bale on top of it. I consider leaving it open so that Ezra could still get out if I don't make it back. Ultimately, I decide against it because, if I don't return, he won't be able to keep his arm from getting infected, meaning he won't make it anyway. I jog up to the door to the barn and crack it open so I can make sure no one is around before I leave. Seeing a clear path, I open the door and make my way out.

The towers of Omaha loom in the distance. Melchior always told us never to go into cities because they weren't safe. Up until now, I had always heeded that advice, but presently I have no other option. I stay off the interstate for as long as I can, still very wary about the fact that our attackers could be anywhere. I bet they were the same ones that came up on us that night a few weeks ago. It's a good thing that they stopped when they did that night or else, we would have been in for a dangerous firefight. I walk through the town of Council Bluff, which has more developed surroundings than the empty plains I am used to, but still only seems to have a few gas stations and old fast-food restaurants. Still, I find these empty buildings where life used to flourish to be incredibly disturbing. It's like seeing the rotting corpse of a civilization. I wish it could be buried and forgotten along with the rest of our sins.

Up ahead I see that I-80 turns into a bridge which crosses the Missouri River. I stop before I get on to the bridge because if I spot someone once I'm up there, I'll have nowhere to hide. I place my hand on the grip of my handgun and remind myself that if I see those two women, I won't hesitate to eliminate them. Content with my surveillance, I start walking up the bridge. It's lucky that it hasn't collapsed because if it had, well, I would be in for quite a long swim. I start getting comfortable, feeling much safer, leaving behind the uneasy apprehension I had when first contemplating going into the city. Fortunately, or I suppose unfortunately, this sense of security I am developing is promptly obliterated once I get to the crest of the bridge. What I see in front of me is a sight that I never expected to see in my entire life. A deer carcass is being eaten by a predator, but it is not just any predator, it is a massive, powerful lion.

I don't even start to consider how or why a lion is in Omaha, but I do take action to ensure that I will not be its next meal. The lion is eating in the far right lane of the bridge, so I quickly sprint over to the far left one, which puts some considerable distance between me and the lion because the bridge has six lanes. I contemplate jumping off the bridge to ensure my safety, but then I think about all the stuff in my backpack that would be completely ruined if I did that. Plus, there's a chance it could jam my weapon and I don't want to be unarmed going into the city. I climb over the railing of the bridge and hang by my hands off the side. The lion is preoccupied with its meal and this way it's unlikely that it will even see me. From a lifetime of rigorous work, the muscles in my arms should be strong enough to let me shimmy along the rest of the bridge. Periodically, I peek my head over the railing to reaffirm that the lion is indeed there. It's been one hell of a day. My arms burn as I traverse the side of the bridge, but I prefer that to the long fall to the water below me. When I make it to the end of the bridge, I feel a wave of relief. The lion is about forty yards away from me now, and if he has noticed me, he doesn't seem to be interested.

I see an alleyway up ahead of me and move towards it as fast as I can, eager to get away from the fleshy death machine behind me. I've never actually been in an alleyway before, so I almost feel claustrophobic in this hall sandwiched between two buildings. It's like being outside but also not being outside. I don't like it at all. On the other side of the alley, I see what appears to be an old bus stop. I walk up to it and see exactly what I was looking for, within a glass casing lies a map of the city of Omaha. When I take a closer look, I understand immediately why there was a lion on the bridge. The Omaha Zoo and Aquarium is only a few blocks down from the bridge I had just crossed. When the Rapture broke out, there must have been no one left to ensure the lions didn't get out of their enclosure. I guess they didn't have any natural predators, so they just kept reproducing. I go back to scanning the map and after about a minute of searching I find exactly what I'm looking for. About a 45-minute walk away by my approximation lies the Omaha VA Hospital. If I'm going to get Ezra some medical supplies, that will be the place to find them. Just as I'm about to leave, I turn back, smash the glass casing with the butt of my pistol, and take the map with me.

I set out immediately with a renewed sense of purpose. On either side of the street the concrete monuments hang over me. It's hard for me to see those skyscrapers as anything other than threatening, although I know that at one point, they used to be a home to someone. As I walk, I periodically hear what sound like gunshots, reminding me that I am not safe here. One day those gunshots will fade, as we won't be able to make bullets anymore. That's something of a comforting thought. What is not comforting, however, is the inevitability of the approaching nightfall. By my measure, it should be getting dark in about an hour or so, which hopefully will give me enough time to loot the hospital and find somewhere to stay for the night. I'm sorry Ezra, but I'm no use to you if I get mauled by a lion on my way back.

After about thirty more minutes of uninterrupted walking, I see the large sign for the VA hospital up on the left. However, I also see that in one of the windows of the hospital, there is an electric light, which likely means that this hospital is not empty. I could try to find another hospital, but with night coming so soon, I wouldn't be able to search for it today. Ezra doesn't have enough time for me to wait until tomorrow to get what he needs. No, if I want to ensure his safety, I have to act now, no matter what the consequences. There's a concrete wall surrounding the hospital's parking lot, but no barbed wire or similar device so I scale it easily. Once I'm on the other side, I stay crouched and walk slowly, weapon in hand, in case I need it. Through the windows on the fourth floor, I can see a person walk past, sending a pang of anxiety through me. I take a deep breath and think of what rides on my actions right now. I will succeed. There is what looks like a maintenance door on the other side of the lot, so I sprint up to it. After checking to make sure I wasn't seen, I take out a screwdriver and bobby pin that I have stored in my bag.

I turn the handle to make sure that it is locked, and upon feeling that it is, I think back to what Melchior taught us about lockpicking. What keeps a lock locked is a series of pins that need to be pushed up just the right amount before the lock can turn. A key has the right corresponding indentations to push up all the pins to turn the lock. By using the bobby pin to push up each pin individually until it clicks into place, and then turning the tumbler with the screwdriver, I can quietly open the lock without the key. After mentally reviewing this process, I execute it swiftly and without error, glad that the muscle memory I developed when Melchior taught us has yet to fade.

I creak open the door to try to keep it from making too much noise. The hallway ahead of me is empty and windowless, only lit by a series of mobile construction lights powered by battery packs. I need to find a map of some kind. What I'm looking for will probably be in the urgent care part of the hospital. I come to an intersection in the hall where I could either turn right or go straight. At first, I start walking to go straight, but then hear garbled voices and footsteps coming from that direction, so I decide to turn. I head down this offshoot hallway for a few steps and find exactly what I'm looking for: a map of the whole facility. From this map, it looks like urgent care is on the third floor. I almost continue down the hall before I realize that the door next to this map has the letters T IRS on it in fading paint, which probably said "STAIRS" in its heyday.

I open the door to find a flight of concrete stairs. Like the rest of the place, it's very dim, as it's only lit by these mobile lantern type lights. The power system for this place is probably completely busted, which I suppose is what happens when it is left unattended for 15 years. I cautiously rise up the stairs, staying low behind the concrete railing so that a person coming from the top wouldn't be able to see me. It is at that moment that my worst fears are realized. I hear a door slam about two levels above me, followed by quick footsteps and an upbeat whistling.

I know what I must do. Stopping right before the staircase turns, I draw my knife. When they come off the staircase coming down, I will jump up, stab them in the neck, and put my hand over their mouth to stop them from screaming. I get nauseous just thinking about what's about to happen. I've fought people before sure, but killed someone? Never. Nonetheless, there will never be a better justification than the one I have now. He's only about five seconds away, I tense my legs and squeeze on the handle of my knife to try to curb the anxiety coursing through my body.

"Damn it, my keys," the man says under his breath in a very exasperated tone.

He turns, and I hear his footsteps begin to move back up the stairs. I wait until I hear the slam of the door on the fourth floor before I start to move. When I do, I dash up the stairs as quickly as I can without making too much of a ruckus. I look through the glass rectangle in the corner of the door to make sure no one is beyond it, and, upon seeing that the coast is clear, I open it and sneak out. I turn left and follow the signs above me that should lead to the urgent care area of the hospital. This place is huge. I can't believe that at one point there were enough doctors to staff this entire hospital. And there were many hospitals in this city. And this city isn't even that big. I've been told what the country's population was before the Rapture, some 300 million or so, but I never really envisioned just how many that was exactly or just how few of us there are left.

I shift my focus back to what is in front of me, using both my eyes and ears to look for signs of activity. Looking out one of the windows to my right I can see that outside the sun is setting, something I knew would occur soon, but it is unsettling, nonetheless. I follow the signs to an intersection in the hallways where it tells me to take a right. I do so and find the place I'm looking for: Urgent Care Storage Room 1 and Urgent Care Storage Room 2. I draw my knife in case there is someone in the rooms, but I highly doubt it since no one would have reason to be there. I open the door to Room 1 and am immensely disturbed by what I find. The entire place has been ransacked and emptied out, and what's left looks like someone's bedroom, complete with posters from pre-Rapture bands and movies. Seeing it forms a pit in my stomach. It reminds me that if I end up hurting one of the inhabitants of this place, I am not hurting an emotionless robot, but a thinking, feeling human being - one with interests and ideas as complex as mine and one who is struggling to stay alive just like me. I feel like too often I manage to separate myself from the raiders and other people, but really, they are just as human as I am. If there is a god, I damn him for what he has done, corrupting the world to the point where we must all struggle against each other to protect the things we love, which only perpetuates our apocalypse rather than solving it.

But I know that under these circumstances, any action to save Ezra is justifiable even if it means taking part in the unjust world, just like the raiders do. If my willingness to take it that far makes me a bad person, then so be it. I would rather be a bad person with Ezra alive than a good one with him dead. I leave this room and give a small prayer to nothing before opening the door to the next one. When I enter the room, I see an empty row of shelving. Behind it I see space for another row. In the corner of the room, I see some mops and brooms, indicating that to some extent the inhabitants of this place use this room as well. I walk through the gap between the first shelf and the wall and turn my eyes to the second row behind it. I scan from top to bottom and for a moment, dread begins to fill me as I don't see what I need. However, in the bottom left corner, I spot two white bags with red crosses on top. I get on my knees and unzip them to make sure that they are not empty. Fortunately, I find that they contain everything I am looking for, from more bandages, to stitches, to antibiotic cream. The kits are large, but they still fit inside my bag. In the corner of the room, I spot something else that's almost as valuable as the supplies: dozens of cans of food. I feel moderately guilty taking ten of them as I can probably survive without them, but we're going to be needing extra food if Ezra can't hunt.

The joy I feel as I find them is just indescribable. It gives meaning to the risk that I am putting on my own life and the lives of those around me. I squeeze between the first shelf and the wall once more in preparation to make my escape. I check the door like usual and exit into an empty hallway. While it is indeed an empty hallway, it did not stay that way for long. Just after I walk out, I hear footsteps coming from another hallway to my left. At first, I try to get back into the storage room, but quickly realize I won't have time, so instead I draw my pistol and aim it at where I expect the man to appear.

He rounds the corner, and it takes him a moment to fully realize what is going on. Before he can run or call for help, I command his attention.

"Don't call your friends or I'll shoot! Drop all your weapons on the ground and go into that closet. I don't want to hurt you, but I will if I have to."

He doesn't respond immediately, but when I look up at his eyes, I don't see the eyes of a man afraid for his life, but rather the mischievous eyes of a kindergartener who knows he's about to do something bad.

Interlude - Apparitions

The dirt clings to me like bugs to a web. The dark surrounds me like an island in the center of a hurricane. The blood coats me like paint on a burning house. Glowing like a crescent moon on a cloudy night, the electric light that lies in my lap is the only thing that lets me keep my sense of self. Barely out of the illuminated area, I sense a faint movement, a jittery dance on the edge of my perception. The silence is as jarring as a train whistle. I don't hear the drip of a leaky pipe or scurrying rats, so when I see this movement, it startles me.

When it finally enters the light, it almost grants me a sense of calm, before I realize that I am helpless against the spider crawling into my lap. I am so drained from the blood loss and shock, the effort of moving my good arm seems too high a cost to pay to eradicate this spider. And even if I could, I could never place my hand back where it belongs, above my wound. Slowly, the spider's tiny limbs begin poking and prodding into my chest as it makes its way up my bloodstained shirt. I've always despised spiders. Everything about them is wrong, from their horrible little mouths to their prying orbs from which they gaze with a cold hatred.

"He's not coming back."

In the silent room, it's almost hard to discern thoughts from speech, so when I hear these words, their origin is unknown to me. I like to think that they came from the spider. All my rage, all my hate, all the malice in my heart can be directed towards this bony arachnid. It's almost as if the strength of my emotions alone would be enough to eviscerate it, but the spider remains unaffected. I lack the strength to weep, but even without physical tears, I mentally sing a song of sorrow greater than I ever have before. And it's selfish, I know. I am alive and those I have lost are not, so they are the ones who deserve sorrow, yet still, those I have lost do not feel the suffering I do. The dead don't have to feel the weight of their own loss.

"He left you behind."

No, he didn't. It hasn't been that long. Has it? The spider crawls onto my neck, with my sensitive skin feeling every touch of the spider's legs. In some deep corner of my mind, I almost wish for it to bite me right there and get me away from this black purgatory. I want to go anywhere or nowhere; I just don't want to be here. But even in this state, the thought of Quinn's mere existence keeps me going. Even if I must suffer I will gladly do it if it means I can be with him. I would suffer a million times more. He will come back. He must come back.

"You're going to die here."

No! No, I'm not. I'm going to live and make it to South Bend. I have to. The spider has crawled onto my check now and is sluggishly moving towards my ear. Right now, I am a mind trapped in a cage, a flesh prison that holds me down, but still, I know that I can make it through this. For a moment I fear the spider is going to crawl into my ear, but luckily it instead leaves my face and clings onto the wall behind me.

Once again, I am truly alone, left to rule over my kingdom of dirt and blood.

Chapter 9 - Quinn

July 13

We stand there in silence for a few seconds, with me staring at him staring at me and my weapon. Suddenly, he starts sprinting back the way he came, shouting, "Jake! Kyle! Cassie! There's an intruder! Get the fucking guns!"

Before he passes out of my view, I have one or two seconds to pull the trigger. But in the moment, I just couldn't bring myself to pull it. I don't have time to chastise myself for my actions, so I start sprinting as fast as I can towards the stairs. The man ran the other way, so I should make it to the stairs before anyone else on this floor has a chance to. The people below us shouldn't be alerted, so I just need to get out before they are. I run as fast as I can without tripping over myself and quickly come to the stairs. I hear shouting coming from behind me, so I open the door, weapon in hand and fortunately find an empty stairway. I try to quickly bar the door behind me, but there's nothing to bar it with, so I begin running down the stairs. My heart is pounding as I run as fast as I can down the three flights of stairs. By the time I reach the bottom without any conflict, I feel unparalleled relief.

As I open the door, however, I quickly find that my relief is premature. A man stands to the right of the door with a revolver aimed right at me. I duck back inside the stairwell just in time, as a bullet erupts from his gun and slams into the concrete where I was just standing. Above me I hear the door to the stairway open, giving me about fifteen seconds before those from above descend upon me. Shit. How did this guy know that I was coming? The bullets keep coming from the man in the hallway, piercing through the now closed door and into the corner of the room. The angle he is shooting from is preventing any of the bullets from hitting me, as I'm standing in the other corner of the room. A plan begins to formulate in my head. Once he fires six shots, I open the door, gun him down, and then sprint away as fast as I can. I count each shot in my head, praying that he finishes before my pursuers catch up to me. Upon hearing the sixth shot, I burst through the door, pointing my gun at his head.

Time seems to almost slow down. At this moment, I have total control over this man's life, and I am going to use that control to end it. I am a monster.

Bang.

Blood spurts out of the hole in his forehead, and he falls onto the ground. I sprint down the hallway, and as I pass by the man's corpse, I see his eyes glazed over, walkie-talkie at his hips, and revolver still clutched in his hand. The gravity of what I have done is yet to hit me, which is probably a good thing; I still need to get out of here. I follow the route I had used to get here. Luckily, I don't see or hear anyone ahead of me, but the death of their comrade will only encourage my pursuers to continue their chase. I make it to the side door I had used to enter and sprint outside, instantly feeling the pouring rain come down onto me. My best bet is to find some alley and hide there, so I run as fast as I can and climb over the concrete wall encircling the entire hospital.

Bang. Bang.

117

Just as I make it to the other side of the wall, I hear two gunshots as bullets fly against the wall I was climbing. That means that they saw which way I went. Shit. It's pitch dark ahead of me because of the rain clouds blocking out the moon. I use my little light to guide me as I run along the sidewalk into the dark, but then realize that it would just turn me into a glowing target once they make it over the wall, so I shut it off. I place my hand on the building next to me and start following it into the nothingness ahead. I feel the smooth wall suddenly stop and turn into open air. I feel the wall around where it stopped for a few seconds and notice that the wall doesn't stop, it just opens up to a window. With my hands, I can feel that the floor on the other side is the same height as the bottom of the window, making me think this was shop before the rapture. I hop through the empty window, careful to not make much noise and alert my pursuers

I quietly lurk deeper into the shop, feeling the floor with my hands to make sure that I don't bump into anything. I think that my pursuers would have made it over the fence by now, but in their frenzy, I doubt that they brought any kind of powerful flashlight. I feel my way to what seems like a low wall of sorts, probably the place where the cash register once stood. Outside the discordant sounds of yelling voices are mostly drowned out by the pouring rain. I should be safe here behind my little wall. As long as it's dark they should have no way of knowing I'm here and even if it wasn't, I don't think I could be seen from the street. I curl up into a ball, my clothes soaked, my principles violated, and my world only held together only by my need to protect Ezra.

I lay in that state for some time, just listening to the rain and occasional thunder. My pursuers are long gone by now, either chasing after me into another part of the city or back in their hospital mourning the loss of their companion. At some point I start crying, but I can't really discern the tears from water dripping down my hair. Even though it's very warm out, the cold rain makes me shiver. I would just go to sleep right there, but the combination of cold and self-hatred keeps me awake. I replay the moment that I killed him over and over in my mind. He had a name, feelings, people who loved him, every prerequisite to be a true human being. And I ended him, I broke into his home and killed him just like the raiders did.

So, there I sit, a broken man in a broken city, left to weep in despair of my own doing.

*   *   *

I don't know exactly when I fell asleep, but it couldn't have been long given the grogginess I feel when I awake. As dawn's first light creeps into my little abandoned store, I thank my ingrained alarm for making sure I can get away before any of the hospital dwellers come and find me. I get up and feel that my clothes are still soggy and gross from last night's rain. Still, I know it is only a small fraction of the discomfort that Ezra is experiencing, which gives me renewed drive to carry on. I peek out the window I came in through and see the hospital down the road, but an otherwise empty street. The sooner I can get away from here, the better.

The second I get onto the street I start jogging, not only to get away from the hospital but also out of my eagerness to reach Ezra. To me, everything about this city is vile and depressing, from the collapsing buildings on either side of me to the cracked concrete below me. It makes me almost wish the apocalypse had come in the form of nuclear annihilation, so that the survivors wouldn't have to stare at their sin like we have to. I think that's why they call it Sin, not because of what it does, but because of what it makes us do. If people just didn't start getting violent towards each other the second something dangerous was on the horizon, then maybe we could have been saved. We could have taken all the remaining untainted food, put it in a large greenhouse, and use it to supply a city like this. There were solutions, we just chose to protect ourselves rather than search for them. Deep down, I know the only reason I'm following this train of thought is because I want an excuse to blame what I've done on anyone but myself. Sin did it… humanity did it… the people chasing Ezra and I did it… all facades, all masks to hide the obvious truth: I'm the one that pulled the trigger.

I'm close to the bridge, probably about five minutes away. All I have to do is cross it and then I will be in the clear. I want to get out of this city and never return more than almost anything else, but as I jog, I stop after every street corner to make sure no one is hiding in wait. After all, I do want to get out of this city alive. I think about Ezra for a moment and a pang of worry flashes through my body. It's been so long; he better be okay. Up ahead I can see the bridge, but what I see is not the escape that I want. Three guards stand poised on the bridge, two looking over either side and one staring straight down the bridge. So that's their strategy, try to catch me as I'm leaving the city. It takes a moment for the gravity of the situation to truly hit me. I have no way of crossing this bridge. I could try to go to the one after that, but they may have people there too. I could go the long way around, but I don't think that Ezra has the time, especially with the amount of food and water that I left him. Is he even strong enough to eat what I left him? It doesn't matter. All that matters is me getting back to him as soon as I can.

I stand behind the corner of a building about a hundred yards away from the bridge. Whenever I look at it, I only peek my eyes out, so they have no way of seeing me. I think that's likely my only advantage, the ability to plan my next move with more information. But unfortunately, I don't think that this advantage will be able to get me out of this one. After a few moments of thinking, I come up with a plan. I will walk down the bank of the river until it's out of sight of the bridges, then I will swim across, keeping the medical supplies at the center of my bag to try to keep them from getting wet. It's not an ideal plan but given the circumstances I don't think I have another option. It's at this moment when a little voice whispers in my ear,

"You could kill them." At first, I downright reject the idea completely. I would never kill someone unless I absolutely had too. And it's not like these people are doing anything wrong, they're just trying to get revenge for their friend. Still, I have to prioritize Ezra's safety above all else here. I would lose so much crossing the river, from damaging my bag, my weapons, and potentially even the supplies I came here to get. I can't let it all be for nothing. But the price I would have to pay to ensure that is just too high. Killing three people? I couldn't. Well, I probably could, if I got to the roof of a building near the bridge, used the remaining four bullets that I have for my rifle, I could probably take them out before they even saw me.

But I can't, right? I'm already a monster, but if I did it, I would be even lower than that. I crash to my knees, utterly crushed by the weight of this decision. I can't. I just can't pick one of the two. If Ezra dies because I was too weak to take the action that would protect him, my life would be over. But if I kill these people to ensure his safety, I imagine I would be left only a husk of my former self. Last time was in the moment. It was the only thing I could do to not die immediately. But this time? It would be pre-meditated, cold-blooded murder.

Bang. Bang.

I hear exactly two gunshots, shortly followed by screaming. I quickly peek around the corner to see what is going on and find a truly shocking situation. The lion that I had seen on this bridge when I first entered Omaha must have charged up the bridge and started mauling the three guards that stood there. The lion is leaking blood from its side due to multiple bullet wounds, but seeing the three shredded men at the lion's feet makes me think that he got the better end of the fight. I turn back behind the wall quickly, as even from this distance, looking at it makes me want to throw up. We are not the apex predators here, and I guess they forgot that. Some inkling of a thought still tries to make me responsible for their deaths because they wouldn't have been there if not for me, but I cannot be responsible for what other people do because of me. If anything, this presents a good opportunity, as once the lion leaves, the path back to Ezra should be clear. However, those gunshots might draw some of the nearby hospital people, which means I need to be ready to go the second the lion no longer poses a problem.

I turn around the corner to see the lion growing disinterested in his half-eaten pile of bodies. He walks back down the bridge and turns left off of it, presumably to go back to the zoo to lick his wounds. I run down the street towards the bridge, sprinting as fast as I can to get out of this god-forsaken city. As I'm on the bridge, I half expect to be shot down by some far away sniper's bullet, ending this tumultuous journey seconds from the end, but fortunately this does not come to pass. After I cross the bridge, I turn back and take a final look at the city from up close. I wish I could forget what happened here, although I doubt I ever will. I always saw this city as a testament to our collective sins, but now, it's a testament to mine too.

I keep following the path back the way I came, jogging as fast as I can without completely depleting my stamina. Ezra's face burns in my mind throughout my entire run. Everything I did is for him, and I know that in some sense, through him I am redeemed. No matter how focused I am, I can't help but get distracted. What pulls my attention is a small boutique bookstore to my left that seems like it hasn't been damaged since the Rapture. I bet a book would be a great gift to Ezra since I doubt, he will be up and about anytime soon. The wood on the door to the store is rotted, so I break it down easily. Inside, the first thing that catches my eye is the checkout desk, where I see some tabloids from about a week before the Rapture. Not forgetting that I'm on the clock, I take a glance at the headline of the front tabloid and read "The Clownery of the Kardashians Ascends to New Heights!" If I wasn't in such a somber mood, I probably would have chuckled.

I quickly start scanning the shelves for a book of interest. Many of them are damaged or inaccessible due to fallen shelves, but I see a shelf in the back of the store that seems to be in pristine condition. I see a number of books here that Ezra might want to read but considering he has never been the most interested in literary matters, I figure that some type of fantasy book would probably suit him best. I search through the books, judging them by their cover due to my limited time. A book with a stark white spine catches my eye. Its title, *The Guild of Oleander*, is written in golden lettering on the front cover. The summary on the back of the book reveals that it is about a group of assassins living in a fantasy world. I think that a fantasy world would do nicely given his current situation. I pick up the book and leave the store as fast as I can, continuing my jog back to the barn.

After a while, the barn passes into my field of vision, lighting a fire under me to run even faster. As I see the side door to the barn, I remember my failure and I'm flooded with embarrassment. At least I got Ezra to safety. I enter the barn and see that the bale of hay lies above the entrance to the cellar just as I left it. After pushing the hay off the hatch, I open it and yell down to Ezra,

"Hey, it's me! I made it back from the city, you alright down there?"

No response. I run down the stairs and take a glance at the cellar but see no light illuminating where Ezra should be. For a moment, I begin to truly break down fearing that all I had done had been for naught.

"Hey, dummy, I'm right here don't worry," I hear Ezra's weak voice call to me.

I turn on my own light and kneel to face Ezra. Careful not to squeeze his wound, I turn and embrace him. With his one good arm, he embraces me back. Now I know for certain, it has all been worth it. I immediately take out the supplies from my bag, as well as one of the cans of beans that I took from the hospital.

"I'm going to re-dress your wound, and then you can eat. Does that sound okay?"

"Yes, doc."

It's good that he is keeping some sense of humor given the circumstances. I open the bandages that I had given him yesterday afternoon. The wound does not seem to be infected yet, which is a good sign. I open up the antibiotic cream and apply it to both the entrance and exit wounds. Ezra winces at times, but I know this is for the best. Afterwards, I take off the rest of the bandages and start to apply the new ones. In the morning I will try to stitch the wound, because I don't think that I'm mentally in the right place to do a procedure like that now.

"Why were you in the dark when I came down here?"

"I couldn't stand to look at this empty room any longer, so I just didn't."

"Well, you won't have to now that I'm here."

"I was so worried about you while you were gone."

"And I was worried about you while you were here."

I lay my head in his lap and he takes his left hand and runs it through my hair. We are both dirty and disgusting from a lack of bathing combined with my damp clothes, but honestly it doesn't matter. We're both still breathing, which in my book is a cause for embrace. After a few minutes I sit up so I can get the canned beans for Ezra to eat. I take them out of my bag, and since I don't have a can opener, I use my knife to break open the lid. I was just about to offer it to Ezra when I realized that I should probably test it for Sin first, even though it is sealed. It's best to be safe. I take a singular bean, slice it, then prick my finger with my knife and wait for a drop of blood to fall onto the bean. It lands square in the center of the black bean and stays there unchanged for the next few seconds.

This all reminds me of Doug's place, which seems like a lifetime ago to me now. It has only been about three weeks, but still, anything before Omaha seems like a distant dream. I bring the beans over to Ezra, along with a spoon, and before they have even left my hands, he begins to devour them. Even when he could use both of his arms, Ezra never ate so fast. I haven't eaten since lunch yesterday but knowing where those beans came from makes me sick at the thought of eating them. Ezra is probably dying to know the origin of the food or medical supplies, but I think he knows that I probably don't want to talk about it. And he's smart enough to see that if I'm not eating, I probably don't want to think about the source of these supplies.

"I'm going to go and refill our canteens. I will be back in a bit," I say, standing up.

Ezra grabs my leg as I'm about to go and pleads, "Come right back once you are done."

"I will."

"Promise?"

"I promise."

*   *   *

The sun has probably set by now, but in our little man-made cave, it's not like we can see it anyway. Ezra managed to stand up, which is a good sign. I managed to make myself eat the beans. I didn't want to leave Ezra alone for as long as it would take to gather something else, and I must eat something eventually. I know I'm just writing these simple facts because I don't want to get to the part of my journal where I have to self-reflect, but hey, at least I'm self-aware. I'm not sure whether to write down the events of Omaha. I can't tell if I want to remember what I've done or forget it completely. No, I have to remember. I can't let myself forget what I've done, otherwise I will subconsciously try to diminish or lessen my sins. I killed a person for personal gain, and at least three more died directly because of my actions. For all my talk about human nature and our rotten soul as a species, really it all comes down to the things and people we want to protect. And that's not selfishness. It's something else in its own right.

I put the journal down and gaze out to the dark room. That's enough of that, I'll get down to writing the rest later. I take off my pants and lay out my sleeping bag, but as I'm putting my pants back in my backpack, I feel the hardcover of *The Guild of Oleander*. Shit! I must have forgot to give him the book in all the confusion of my return. Better late than never, I guess.

"Hey, I found this on my way back and thought you might want it. I know you've never been the most into reading, but it's not like you have much else to do."

Ezra sits up in his sleeping bag and says, "I suppose I can look before I go to sleep. What's it about?"

"A group of assassins trying to overthrow an evil empire. Typical YA stuff."

"Sounds mindless. I like it."

"Well that's it for me. I'm hitting the sack. Don't stay up too late reading."

"I probably won't. Sweet dreams."

"Sweet dreams."

The Guild of Oleander - Archeon

863 A.T.R

I send my sword flying through the adamantine gate leading to the Archinquisitor's quarters. He will be the final trial, the final seal, all that stands between me and the Holy Arbiter. The blade comes to a sudden halt only millimeters in front of the gate. I force more mana through the link between my blade and me. It's not that I am running out of power, as the hate I feel is strong enough to provide all the energy I require, but it almost seems as if I am trying to drain an ocean with a straw. No matter how much force I put behind the floating longsword, it remains stationary, held back by the strong warding on the door. I recall my blade back to my hand. If I can't channel it through my blade, then a pure release of mana should be able to level the gate. The others at the guild say that releasing pure mana is as likely to damage yourself as much as your target, but this isn't important to me right now given the circumstances. I pour as much mana as I can directly into my hand. From behind me I hear the chaos of the siege, the clash of swords and screams of dying men, giving me even more motivation to succeed. They fight and die so that I have the chance to win.

I feel the mana pour from my core into my left hand, this time not as through a straw but a waterfall. It takes all my energy to hold back the mana from escaping my hand until I have enough stored to blow through the warding. It all comes down to me, to this moment. If I fail, the tyranny of the Arbiter will reign for centuries more at the least. I finally think that I have enough energy charged to take out the warding, so with a scream I let it all out. Pure energy springs from my palm, burning with the brightest white I have ever seen. For the first second, my arm burns with unimaginable pain, but it almost instantly blinks away. I thank Estra for my artificial eyes, as any normal ones would be instantly blinded by this light. This is only a fraction of my power. The Archinquisitor will melt before me.

The light fades and in front of me glows the molten edges of the door, with its inner portion being completely vaporized. It takes a moment before I realize that the door is not the only thing that has been obliterated. My entire arm past my elbow is completely missing, but the heat from the release of mana seems to have cauterized the wound, so it won't hinder me too much. I sprint through the door, noticing the corpses of inquisitors that were melted by the burst. The hallway curves to the right, and as it does, I see a dozen inquisitors standing poised, two by two, ready to stop my advance. I consider sending another pure mana blast, but I can't risk losing my other arm. I guess I will have to do this the old-fashioned way.

With my blade in my right hand, I charge at my crimson-clad enemies. As I approach, one swings his glaive with superhuman speed, but I slide under it with ease. Throwing up my blade at the last second, I slide under his legs. Once I have emerged on the other side of him, I summon my floating blade through his chest, cross guard and all. The inquisitor standing next to the one I just slew slashes down, trying to kill me before I even have the chance to stand. The hilt of my sword emerges from the previous man's chest just in time for me to grasp it and parry the blow coming towards me. I leap up before he even has the chance to recover his footing, and with one smooth motion I slice through the neck joints in his armor, sending his head rolling down the hall. The blood of my opponents clings to the blade of my weapon as a thick fluid, dyeing it the same color as my opponent's armor. I point the tip of my blade at my next targets, and they silently start sprinting at me, each armed with two small daggers, poisoned no doubt. I let just a drop of mana flow into my blade and as it does, the blood coating my blade crystalizes and explodes in a cone towards the inquisitors. Too close to erect a mana shield, the hundreds of sanguine shards shred them to pieces. The ones behind them, however, do manage to block the projectiles.

Slowly walking towards them, I let my blade fall from my hand and hover upright in
front of me. Without breaking my stride, I send my weapon flying towards the woman on the right at twice the speed of a standard arrow. She manages to bring her blade up to block just in time, but the force of the impact is enough to send it flying from her hand. I start to swing my blade at her throat, but her partner swings down with his to knock my sword off its trajectory. I twirl my blade at the last second so his strike meets nothing but air and then send it around, so its tip is pointing at his side. I launch it forward and skewer both onto the wall. They don't even cry out in pain as life fades from their eyes. They just stare at me silently, surely making a wordless prayer to the Holy Arbiter.

I call my blade back to my hand and thrust it into the ground. The pool of blood around the blade begins to shift and crystalize into the shape of a dire wolf. I yank my blade out of the ground and the ruby wolf howls a high-pitched cry before sprinting at my targets. It leaps toward the man on the left and rips his throat out before he can even react, and then jumps onto the chest of his partner, forcing her to the ground. In her final moments, she manages to jam a knife into the wolf's neck as it finishes her off. The wolf de-crystallizes, covering the woman in the blood of her comrades.

The next pair silently charges at me. These inquisitors have no art in their movements. They are so used to overpowering their opponents through pure strength and speed that they forsake any creative thinking. Though I suppose they don't need creative thinking when their mana-infused abilities are enough to defeat any normal warrior. It's a good thing that I'm no normal warrior. As I wait for these next opponents to reach me, I surge mana into my right arm and poise my blade ready to make a horizontal slash. Just as they come in reach, I release the mana in my arm, sending it and the blade it holds towards the inquisitors. The attack was incredibly telegraphed, so both already had their blades up to block, but the sheer force of the attack slices through both of their blades, rending both inquisitors clean in two. The momentum they are running with carries their bodies forward.

The last two inquisitors both draw their bows, seemingly unaffected by the deaths of all the rest of their comrades. Inquisitor battalions, especially ones as elite as the Seraphs of the Dark, have lived their entire lives together, raised to be battle brothers and sisters from the moment they are stolen from their parents. I can't understand how they can lose everything without giving even the slightest reaction. Regardless, the pain of their loss will soon end once

I finish off the remaining Seraphs. The two arrows charged with mana come flying towards me at hundreds of miles per hour, but I dodge them without trouble. I hear the explosion that results from the force of the arrows hitting the wall. I'm only a few feet from the archers now, but they manage to fire off one more volley before I reach them. I don't have enough time to dodge now, so I throw up a shield of mana. The arrows silently slam into the shield of energy and fall to the ground after all the force behind them is drained. The last two inquisitors know by now their death is assured, yet I don't see a glimmer of fear in their eyes. For as much as I hate them, some part of me respects them too. I end these last two with a swift slash across their chests. My blade is almost heavy with blood now, so I crystalize it with my mana and send it sliding over the vulnerable parts of my armor in preparation for my fight with the Archinquisitor.

I walk through the stone arch connecting the hallway into an empty common room used by the Seraphs of the Dark. On one of the tables in the center of the room I see a chess board left in the middle of the game. Even as the walls of Halcyon come crashing down, the Seraphs just played games. Typical. I expected the Archinquisitor to be waiting here for me, but I suppose he must be waiting by the Arbiter. There are seven hallways leading out from the common room, excluding the one that I just came through. The one directly in front of me likely leads to the Arbiter's chamber, as it seems much wider than the others. Knowing I have no time to waste, I start running towards the hall, but at the last second, I realize my mistake. I turn and raise my blade as fast as I can, barely knocking the Archinquisitor's kunai off its deadly trajectory. The Archinquisitor himself is quick to follow his projectile, jumping down from a nook in the ceiling.

He travels with speed comparable to mine. He's the Empire's deadliest warrior after all, but I am able to match blades with him, halting the fatal arc of his katana. I swing my foot around to try to break his stance, but he leaps back before my attack can connect. The Archinquisitor is a skinny but tall man dressed in all black garb, sharply contrasting my white and amber outfit. The other Oleanders told me that the Archinquisitor used to be one of us, but after confronting the Arbiter something happened to him. They said his name is Tanvir, though I doubt he has been called that in years. For all the destruction I have wrought against the Empire, I have never fought him before, as he stays glued to the Arbiter to ensure that no harm comes to him.

"Tanvir, if you're still in th-"

He lunges at me with a speed that doesn't give me enough time to block or raise a shield. I shift an amber shard to where I believe his blade will strike, and fortunately, my approximation was correct. The strength of the blow still knocks me back and slams me against the wall, but the now-shattered amber protected me from any mortal injury. Tanvir follows up with a leaping slash, but I duck under the blade which cuts through the stone wall behind me like butter. I try to hurl my blade to impale him in the stomach, but he recovers from his previous strike fast enough to knock my blade off course, causing it to pierce the ceiling rather than my enemy. I command my blade to return to my hand, but Tanvir is faster, arcing a strike straight to my gut. Once again, I lack the speed to dodge or a weapon to block with, so I send all my amber shards to where his blade will connect. The shards all shatter with a high-pitched crack, but I don't feel the warm drip of blood across my stomach, so I know they did their job. My blade comes down from the ceiling aiming directly at Tanvir's head. He prepares another strike towards me, thinking to finish me as I am forced against the wall. At the last moment he realizes his threat from above and tries to swing his head out of the way. He is only partly successful as my blade grazes his cheek, sucking blood from the wound and onto my blade as it does.

It then arrives in my hand, leading me to make a waist level swing at my opponent. He leaps back, trying to get some distance between us so he can start his assault anew. I don't let up the pressure, crystalizing some of the blood on my blade and flinging it back at him with devastating speed. He parries them with equal speed before leaping back towards me. To keep from being pressed against the wall, I leap forward to meet him in the middle. From there we exchange a flurry of blows, with neither of us being able to get the upper hand. To an outsider, our attacks and parries would be almost invisible due to the speed at which we fight, but to us, our artificial eyes allow us to track objects at the rate at which our mana lets us move. Seeing the futility of these attacks, I leap to the side, careful not to back myself into a corner. Tanvir and I circle each other, eyeing for any weakness in the other's form. I consider trying to send my blade towards him, but likely he would just dodge and attack me before I could recall it. I still have enough blood for one more maneuver, but I'm not sure how to capitalize on it given the fact he's just as fast as me. Tanvir decides to attack, so I lunge forward to engage him.

It takes all my focus to avoid getting hit while still making attacks of my own. Given my lack of progress, I decide to make a reckless attack, one that will be hard for Tanvir to block, but if he does, I won't have time to block his next jab. My blade curves towards his left side, but with abnormal speed, even for him, he maneuvers his katana to block it. Seeing this opening, he pierces into my left side, causing a shooting pain, beyond what I expected. However, as he jabs, I crystalize the remaining blood on my blade into a small dagger that I fling towards Tanvir's neck as fast as I can. Tanvir realizes my trap, but at this point it's already too late for him to do anything. The dagger pierces him under his chin and comes shooting out the top of his skull, finally shattering when it hits the ceiling. His lifeless body collapses to the ground, leaving his katana still impaled through my torso. I grab it with both hands and tug as hard as possible, a scream leaving my body with the blade. Normally, I could heal this kind of wound with relative ease, but unsurprisingly there is something on the blade that is preventing me from doing so.

I take the katana and use it as a crutch so I can make my way to the Holy Arbiter, with my sword hovering beside me ready to dispatch any enemies that could be hiding. I hobble down the marble hallway, looking at the elegant portraits of the Arbiter, dating from various times since the rebirth. In each one he is portrayed as a giant, hulking man, covered in golden armor and wielding a massive sword. I haven't read the Texts since I was a boy, but I would imagine that these paintings portray the major events in them. In one, the Arbiter stands above a jungle of concrete towers as they are wiped away by a massive tsunami. Seeing them makes my blood boil with hatred, not only for the Arbiter but for the Empire he created. If he is blessed with this godlike power, then why does he execute or recruit all mana users? Why does he allow most citizens to live in cramped hovels while the nobles enjoy lives of luxury and excess? If he is so right, then why is the world so wrong?

The door to his chamber is mere meters away, but my wound keeps me from running to it. I'm sure he is going to give me some speech to try to stop me from killing him, but I'm not going to listen. The second that door opens I am going to send my sword to chop off his head. I arrive at the door and prepare to do another mana blast with my good arm, but I hear a click and it slowly begins to open. I move in as fast as possible, prepared to see a towering, angelic figure. Instead, I see a weak old man bound to a small metal throne. The room we are in has large, reinforced windows overlooking the battlefield, but no off-shooting hallways. I prepare to execute him, but then realize there is a possibility this isn't the real arbiter, but rather a fake.

"Are you the Holy Arbiter?"

"You took longer than expected, Archeon."

I send my sword to his throat before saying, "Give me an answer"

"I know you want to kill me, not without good reason, but consider this, if I had the power to stop you, I would have done so, so what is the harm in giving me a simple conversation?"

"Goodbye, Arbiter."

"Don't you want answers?"

Those simple little words kept my blade from entering his throat. I do want answers, more than almost anything else. And like he said, if he could stop me, he would have.

"What is the truth about mana and the Rebirth?"

"Years prior to the rebirth, the earth was dying; natural resources were running dry and hundreds of millions of people were being displaced by rising tides. Certain governments thought that if they could somehow eliminate the populations of other countries without destroying their land, all the people they governed would have enough to live on. They ended up beginning production of ARC, which in theory would be dispersed into the atmosphere, spreading out and killing all of those that didn't have the vaccination, which the government would give out to its people under the guise of a regular vaccine for common illnesses. It was a crazy plan, but desperate times called for desperate measures. But the person who designed ARC was lying to the government. He thought that life on earth didn't deserve to continue, so just before ARC was released, he tampered with the formula so that it would neutralize all life on earth. I was the head of another government project at the time, the M.A.N.A project which hoped to rescue the country from its dire straits not by killing all others, but by imbuing certain individuals with an ability to manipulate energy. The project was cancelled after the government decided that ARC was a better alternative and that my plans were nothing but a pipe dream. Well, on the same day ARC was being launched, I completed the equation that was the key to mana. Instantly, I was granted greater power than any petty mana user today. I traveled to the lab where ARC was produced, defeating any security with ease. When I realized not only that it had been released, but had been altered in such a way, I knew I had only one possible choice, to set all my mana to preserve the world in face of the deadly chemical falling upon us. With all my mana tied up in preserving my body and this planet, I imbued others with its power, albeit a weaker version, and forged this Empire from the ground up as the rest of the world collapsed under the ongoing ecological decay. That is the truth of the Rebirth!"

"You've lost your mind. You expect me to believe any of that? The Texts were all lies, that I knew, but you are offering me that bullshit as an answer? I should never have listened to you."

"Some details I may have embellished or shifted for dramatic effect, that I will admit. But the heart of the story is true. Look what happens when I remove my protection from a mana-less lifeform."

In an instant, the trees and grass surrounding Halcyon fade to brown and wilt. No, it can't be. There's just no way he can be telling the truth. It's not possible. All this work, everything I have done, for it all to be for nothing, I can't abide that.

"But still, if you had all this power, why did you build such a cruel and vile Empire?"

"Well, for my people, I built a wonderful Empire. It just so happens that our needs are opposed to those of your people."

"What?"

"Tribalism, class conflict, whatever you want to call it. People look out for their own. But that's unimportant. What matters is that I get to decide, since, as I've already stated, this world only exists by my grace. So now you have a choice: Kill me and let the world die with me. Your mana should protect you for a while, but soon you would run out of things to eat so, well, you wouldn't last long. Or you can become my new Archinquisitor and help me restore the Empire you destroyed."

This must have been the same choice he forced on Tanvir to make him change sides.

"What if, instead of that, we imprison you and force you to keep the world going?"

"I would simply let the world die and then start over. I have more than enough enough mana to start life anew."

"Well then, what if I just leave? I will never work for you!"

"Then, I will end it anyway. I get what I want, and what I want is for you to make this choice. Now be quick about it!"

I can't. I just can't. It's an impossible choice to either kill everyone or continue perpetuating the suffering that an average person deals with every day. I can't- I absolutely can't. But as much as I can't choose, I still must. I grit my teeth and stare into the Arbiter's eyes.

"I-

Chapter 10 - Ezra

July 17

Noooooooooooooooo!"

Quinn sits up in his sleeping bag and reaches for his weapon before saying, "What's wrong? Did they find us?"

"No, no, it's just I made it to the end of that book you gave me, but the last few pages are covered in mold so I can't find out how it ends!"

"It's like three in the morning, Ezra. Have you done anything but read since I gave it to you?"

"I've done plenty, ranging from staring at the wall, to eating, to talking with you and absolutely nothing else because I can't leave this fucking place."

"Is the book even any good?"

"Not particularly. The ending was a little convoluted, but it was unexpected. It was fun though, that's for sure. I'm just annoyed that I won't be able to see the proper ending of it unless we find another copy somewhere."

"I'm sorry, Ezra. I wouldn't have gotten that book if I had realized it was damaged. It looked like it wasn't since it came from the undamaged section, but I guess I was wrong."

"Don't worry, it's not the end of the world. Plus, the book was still enjoyable, and it gave me something to do for the past few days."

"Well, you should probably go to sleep now. You don't want your sleep schedule to be too messed up for when we start going back to our travels.

"I suppose. Well, goodnight."

"Goodnight."

Quinn is right, I really should go to sleep. But I can't help but think back to Archeon's escapades. To have that kind of power, but still be rendered helpless, I couldn't imagine that. I don't really know what I would have picked in his situation. I mean, I think it would be better to just avoid continuing the suffering of so many people, but would I really be willing to be the person to end not only all of humanity, but all life on earth? It's obviously a ridiculous scenario, but still, it's interesting to think about. Maybe I will ask Quinn to get me another book before we leave here since I doubt that I will be ready to leave for at least a few more days.

For a moment I wonder if Sin was artificially made like ARC was. Based on what we read about Ichthys and their talk of "The Egg," I feel like it wasn't something they made themselves, although they did claim that they were responsible for Sin. I'm sure Quinn and I will get some answers when we make it to South Bend. What I really wish would happen is that we find some clearly evil villain who can explain the whole mystery in detail before we punish them for their deeds and save the world. I want to have an ending as clear as *The Guild of Oleander*, but minus the shitty ultimatum. But this is real life, not a book, so I doubt that I will get anything resembling that kind of conclusion.

* * *

July 22

As I open the door to the barn with my good hand, I am almost blinded by the sunlight. I've been outside before during my stay at the wonderful "hotel musty basement," but still it feels so good to be away from the room's oppressive darkness. However, leaving the basement does bring the fear of another surprise bullet taking me down for good this time. It's possible that the shooter is still lying in wait around here, just hoping for the right opportunity to blow my brains out. It's also possible that the shooter was just a random person who wanted to steal our shit. There's really no way to know, but we do know that we can't just stay in that basement forever, meaning that it's time to hit the road.

Quinn follows me out the door, eyeing our surroundings uneasily. I can't pinpoint it exactly, but ever since he came back from Omaha, he's had a sort of edge to him that just won't go away. He has just been practicing knife throwing with this empty look in his eyes, repeating the same motion over and over. I won't ask what's wrong, because I'm sure that he will open up to me soon enough. As we walk back towards I-80, I feel that even the dry heat of the summer sun is a welcome replacement for the unmoving and empty basement. Thinking back to the basement drives my mind towards the people that put us there. I'm sure that in their own minds they were justified in their actions, just as I have been justified in mine. Even after all I've been through, I still feel that at heart, we as people are social beings and instinctively look out for each other. When we take actions not in accordance with that principle, for the most part it's because we are blinded by a strong emotion of some kind. I have to keep believing that. Otherwise, what's the point in hoping that this world even survives?

As we make it to the road, we agree to walk along its wooded edge rather than in the center as we had in the past. We may still be targets, but we might as well make it as hard for them as possible. Assuming that everything goes relatively smoothly, we should be about halfway to South Bend now. As it gets closer, I remind myself that it's a real place and not just some idealistic destination that only exists to be spoken about. I think about how anticlimactic it would be if we make it to the address and the building is just rubble now. What would we even do? Would we just go back to Colorado? It's still too far in the future for me to seriously consider, because even though I don't have any evidence to support it, I believe that we are going to find something important in South Bend. Even as we walk through the bland plains of Iowa, I feel good. Maybe it's just the sun or the wind at my back, but for some strange reason, I am in a really, really good mood.

My wounded arm constantly throbs as I walk, but it's not that much more painful than it was just sitting. As I look out at the road ahead of me, I'm inspired by a strange sense of… hope? Maybe "purpose" is a better term. Up until now, Quinn has been about the only thing that made life worth living to me, but seeing what's ahead, even though I have no idea if it's good or bad, I feel that not only do I want to experience it, but I need to. Not for anyone else, but purely for myself. This sensation will probably fade as time progresses, but seeing what I was missing in that basement has given me a willingness to live beyond what I could have imagined.

*   *   *

July 29

The road takes its toll, as it always does. In the coming horizon we see a city, which immediately sets Quinn on edge. When we find some area to settle down after South Bend, it certainly cannot be near any cities, that's for sure. This particular city is Des Moines, and luckily, I-80 doesn't run straight through it, so I anticipate we will be fine. Still, the gloom that defines Quinn's face is unmistakable, so I figure I should try to give him something to think about other than whatever demons are haunting him.

"What would you say your favorite thing is?"

"Favorite thing?" he questions back, puzzled but intrigued.

"Yeah, favorite thing, like favorite object or concept that you know of. It can be for whatever reason, like beauty, aesthetic, purpose whatever."

"What do you mean by concept?"

"Like the smell after it rains or the feeling of a long night's rest. It's just something intangible.

"I see, I see. I'm still stumped though. Do you want to answer first?"

Well, my obvious answer is Quinn. Everything about him is just perfect, from his distinctive scent to his low tone of voice to his beautiful body. He makes me happy just by existing. But I can't say any of that, for as much as I love Quinn, I fear losing him too.

"Aside from your companionship, I would probably say being in a cozy place during a stormy night. The feeling of being safe and comfortable when outside is all wet and cold - that's just the best."

While he tries to hide it, I can see that for some reason saying that made him make the smallest grimace. I hope I didn't say anything wrong.

"As you know, I'm not a huge fan of storms in the first place, but I agree it's nice to be sheltered from them. My favorite thing, other than your company, is a nice crisp sunny day. Unless things are otherwise really bad, being outside when the weather is in that sweet spot where it's kind of chilly, but perfect in the sun, just boosts my spirits by default. Today isn't like that, unfortunately. But fall is coming soon at least, that should be something to happy about, right?"

"We still have to make it through this summer, but yeah when we get to those nicer temperatures it's definitely going to make things better. But then alas, we have winter which as usual will suck so much. Could you imagine if we had found that facility in the winter, so we would know about South Bend but be unable to go searching for it until winter ended? That wou-"

"Wait a minute, what is that down the road there?"

I look in the direction that Quinn identified and see something that looks like a small pylon. But there's something off about it, it seems like the outline of a person is hanging off the front side of it.

"Let's be cautious for now. I don't know for certain what that is down there, but I do know that I don't like it," I state while checking my surroundings for any immediate danger.

We crouch through the long grass and as we approach the true horror of the situation reveals itself. The thing that I thought was a pylon is actually a cross, and the human figure is a man nailed to it. From what I can tell, the man is still alive but has been there for some time. His eyes are barely open and his head droops downward. His skin is peeling from exposure to the sun and his body is covered in bruises. He looks completely broken. I've seen a lot of cruelty in my life but this - this is something different. To cause so much pain in another human being is just unimaginable to me.

"Come on, let's get off the road for now, and we come back to it when we are safely away from Des Moines," Quinn whispers.

"No. We can't just let him suffer there. I doubt we will be able to help him really, at this point he is as good as gone, so we might as well put him out of his misery so he isn't left to rot here."

"Ezra, come on, he's on the way out anyway, but we are very much in the land of the living. We should get out of here now"

"If we do nothing, what separates us from them?"

"I didn't crucify a person!"

"But we would be complicit in letting it continue."

"Fine, I'll stay here and watch out for anyone approaching. And do it with a knife, we don't want anyone to hear us."

I nod and slowly walk out from behind the bramble. The man seems to partially acknowledge my existence, but doesn't bother to lift his head up to look at me.

"Have you come," he heaves, pausing between each word, "To punish me too?"

"No, I'm here to end your punishment."

"Thank you," he groans, ending with a harsh cough. I bet he hasn't spoken much recently and is likely very dehydrated.

I grab my hunting knife from its holster at my side. This is going to be nasty, but I know that it's the right thing to do. In this case, death is the only mercy I can give him. Normally, I could do this quietly with a bow, but looking at the state of my left arm, which still lies in a splint, that option is closed off to me. Considering how high he is nailed up there, I can't just cut his throat, which would end him relatively quickly. I could try to chop him down, but I wouldn't want to cause him any undue suffering. I think the only option left is for me to throw my knife, then cut down the cross to retrieve it. This just means that I can't miss, not that I ever would after those long training sessions with Melchior. I decide not to tell him what I am going to do, as the anticipation of it would only make it worse for him. I grip my knife, making sure to leave space between the edge of my hand and the start of the blade.

Putting in a strong amount of force, I launch my blade with a half-spin throw. The man grunts before going silent as it implants itself in the center of his forehead, just where I was aiming. I kneel before the man I have just slain and give him a moment of silence before I come and ask Quinn to chop down the cross. I look at the man's strung-up body and a single tear runs down my cheek as I do. I don't think Archeon would be wrong if he killed the Arbiter. Not that he would be right, but I don't think he would be wrong either. To see this and still believe that we deserve to exist takes a strength of will that I don't think that I have right now.

I walk back to the bushes where Quinn crouches, weapon in hand and say, "I need your hands, can you help me cut down the cross so I can get my knife?"

He nods his head and stands up. The cross is held up by four ropes on either side. If we cut those and give it a good push, it should come down pretty easily. Quinn uses his own knife to cut the ropes, but I can clearly see that the entire time he does so he never even glances up at the body. He looks quite out of it, not just in the sense that he's upset that we're stopping in a dangerous area, but also that what he's seeing disturbs him deeply. With the last rope cut, a light push sends the cross tumbling to the ground. I walk over and take my blade out from the man's head, avoiding looking at his gory wound as I do. I wipe the blood off my blade against the side of the cross. I consider asking Quinn if we can take him off of the cross and bury him, but realistically we shouldn't stay here if we know that there are groups that would do something as horrendous as this. I wonder if cities were this much worse than the country before the apocalypse.

"Come on, let's get out of here," Quinn calls to me sharply as he starts to walk away.

Wordlessly, I follow behind as he crosses the derelict road and into the plains beyond. Really there isn't much to say after what he has just seen and what I have done. I look down and gaze at my steel hunting knife. I hold no regrets about what I have had to do with this; I only regret the circumstances that made me have to use it. I pick up the pace a little bit so I can walk next to Quinn instead of behind him. He looks pensive. I never did ask him about what happened in Omaha. I thought it might be better to give him time to think it over and eventually move on, but I don't see that happening. Ever since he got back, he's been different. He's always a little spaced out when I try to talk to him; he just seems to smile less and grimace more.

I let him stew for a few minutes as we walk, but I assure myself that I will talk to him at some point soon. It's my duty as his companion to protect him in all ways, and that includes from himself.

That moment comes about ten minutes later, when I finally muster the courage to speak up.

"Quinn, you know that you can always talk to me about anything, right?

"Okay..." he replies without even looking at me.

"I can see something has been bothering you ever since you got back from Omaha. I'm here for you, Quinn, no matter what it is. I'm just trying to support you. I get that sometimes the guilt can be hard to man-"

"Look Ezra, just because I'm not some emotionless robot like you doesn't mean there's anything wrong with me. Now, can you please just leave me alone?"

His words hurt like a hot iron pressing against my chest. I know he's only lashing out in pain, but still, I can't help but feel the burn from his cruel words. I could take cruelty from anyone but him. It just breaks me on a fundamental level. I think seeing that man and seeing me kill him really set something off within him, because before, while he had an air of gloom, he was still mostly himself. Now though, he just looks like a tormented husk of who he was. That's probably too harsh of a diagnosis, but the issue remains. Clearly what I have just done has triggered something within him, and it just hurts to see the one I love in so much pain. It makes a hatred for those that shot me burn even stronger in my gut. Violence is violence, but they fucked with his mind. That, I can't forgive.

*   *   *

We didn't speak for the rest of the day, continuing our journey across the wastes in complete silence. As we start building our fire to cook the goods that we've gathered today, Quinn finally speaks. I can see before he even starts that he's guilty about what he said earlier today.

"Ezra, we both know that I said something I didn't mean. It's just, I don't understand how you do it so easily. Deal with what you've done, I mean. Because it tears at me moment after moment no matter what I do, and when I see you live so unburdened... it's just hard for me. And I don't like this, us being mad at each other, so I want to apologize and maybe... talk about it?"

I knew that an apology like this was inevitable. What he said came from hurt, not his heart, but initially I had planned to stand my ground a little bit before I completely capitulated. Looking into those pure eyes of his, I know I can't help but accept his apology immediately.

"Trust me, I know you didn't mean what you said, and I forgive you. And I do get it, dealing with the guilt of what you have done is never easy. I've always been able to move past it quickly, but the things you do stick with you, always. I shouldn't have done what I did today in your plain view, and I shouldn't have tried to pester you about it after. For that I'm sorry too."

The two of us come together for a long embrace. I think that maybe, when this is all over, I might just ask him if we can be together. After all we have been through, especially over the past two months, even if he says no, I feel like we can work past it.

"Do you want to talk about any of it, what happened in Omaha I mean?

"No, not really. But I would appreciate it if you could give me some advice on how to handle the guilt."

"There's no one answer to that, but I suppose I can give you my thought process. You're going to spend a lot of time trying to decide whether what you did was justified. To you, it was. To the families of those we have hurt, nothing can justify it. Killing someone is a vile thing that has vile consequences. There is nothing redeemable in the act itself But I know that every time I have, I was willing to cause that pain to prevent something I considered worse from happening. And beyond that, what's done is done. But I know that if I could go back in time, I would make the same decision over again. Life is cruel and often are instruments of that cruelty, but I know that both you and I only do what we have to survive. In that I find solace."

"Thank you, Ezra. There will be no miracle cure, as I'm sure you know, but it's a start."

The rest of the night goes by quickly. We eat, talk, and laugh before getting ready to go to sleep. Today wasn't great, but I think something really important happened, so overall, it wasn't too bad either.

Chapter 11 - Quinn

As we walk along the interstate, we see a worn and rusted sign that reads "E ter ng Illin s." It looks like after months of travel; we are only one state away from our objective. It's probably about two weeks away at best, but the prospect of it has both of us brimming with excitement. Ezra notices the sign as well, stopping me to talk. He pulls out the drawing of the map of South Bend that he copied back in Colorado.

"Quinn, from here it seems like we have two options. We can either take the longer route, turning at the intersection of I-39, head south until we reach the town of Bloomington, then head east and turn back north at Crawfordsville. Or we could just go straight and head through Chicago, which would save us some-"

"The other one. No cities."

"No cities it is."

As we walk down the empty road, we both flash each other the occasional smile. Nearing the end of a journey is always something to be celebrated, especially when something so momentous lies at the end of it. The day is calm and clear, and while the summer sun beats down on us with unparalleled radiance, we honestly don't mind too much. By the end of the day, we had turned off I-80 for the first time in our long expedition. I-39 wasn't too different in practice, but knowing it is a new road makes a substantial difference mentally. It gives a sense of progress.

Good things are going to come. I can feel it.

* * *

August 9

The town of Bloomington is about as bland as abandoned old towns can be. Realistically, it's large enough to be considered a city, but in my opinion lacks the sinister quality of places like Omaha. Still, Ezra and I make sure that we skirt the edges of the place rather than barge straight through it. Using our compass, we end up making our way onto I-74, which we will follow all the way to Crawfordsville. Looking out across the plains around us and the road ahead, I feel comfortable.

"What do you think we should do after this if we get to South Bend and it's a dead end?" Ezra questions.

"Well, I suppose we could head further north. Wasn't there a joke about Canadians being overly nice?"

"Yeah, I think so, although I imagine that winters would be even colder if we went further north than Colorado."

"Colder winters always come with fewer people, meaning less danger and more food."

"True, true. For now, I think we should still act on the assumption that we are going to achieve some wonderful revelation in South Bend."

I nod my head. I'm covered in sweat, but I am still enjoying the trek.

In the distance, I can see a gas station with a destroyed roof. The paint on all the walls is incredibly chipped, leaving only the bare exterior. As we approach, it starts to look as if there is something on the ground. No, not something, but someone. It looks as if there is dried blood across his chest, but even from this distance we can see that he is still alive. I'm apprehensive of course, as I don't want this to turn into a similar situation as that crucified man earlier. Unfortunately for us, it soon becomes much worse.

The gas station appears empty, and the surrounding plains are abandoned, so we head towards the man without taking too many precautions for our own safety. This is a mistake By the time we are about ten feet away from the man, I notice that the red that I had assumed was blood was just red paint atop the man's jacket. By that point I know something is wrong, so I reach for my pistol, but before I can the man sits up and points a revolver at us. I haven't even touched my weapon yet, so I slowly put my hands on my head hoping this is a simple robbery. Soon after this, I see about six more men emerge from within the old gas station. Each of them is wearing a letterman jacket with the word "Cavaliers" printed on it and the logo of a man on a horse. That probably means this is some kind of gang. This is bad. Really bad.

"Put your weapons on the ground and slowly release your backpacks," the formerly wounded man orders.

Ezra and I have no choice but to obey. I glance over at Ezra's face and see something that's usually missing from his eyes: fear. True fear. We kick over our weapons and supplies to the men. If all they are doing is taking our stuff, it will set us back, but Melchior ensured that we could survive in the wilderness. Our captors, however, have plans other than simple thievery.

"Turn around and put your hands behind your back!" the man orders aggressively.

We do as he says once more. The second that I feel the zip ties close around my wrists, a sense of dread sets upon me. I've seen all the disgusting shit that happens to helpless people in this world. Crucifixion and cannibalism. These are the fates I see laid out before me. Even worse, I see these as the fates laid out for Ezra as well. With that notion, I feel a primal rage deep inside me. I want to slaughter all these men with everything I have, tear them limb from limb for the distress they have caused us. But the fact remains, they are the ones with guns, not us. We are the captives. And as is often the case, there is no knight in shining armor to come save us.

Threatening us with their weapons, they force us to walk off I-39 for about a mile. We arrive upon what looks like a military transport truck with the back cover removed. There are probably about ten other people bound up in this transport as well. I doubt they would use the precious resource of gasoline if we are mere human sacrifices, so that gives me some comfort. If we are to die anyway, I think I might just start a ruckus and go out in a blaze of glory, but as things are now, there's still some hope that we can make it out alive, so I will play the part of the passive captive. While our hands are still in zip ties, they attach wooden bracelets to our wrists. The bracelet is composed of several wooden beads with a hole in the middle run through by a thick string. I notice that on Ezra's bracelet, there is a long wooden rectangle where the number 3762-2 is engraved. In front of me, I see them carve the same number onto the outside of his bag using a knife. Why would they need to know that his bag belongs to him? Aren't they just going to steal it?

They herd us on the transport, where we end up sitting facing each other on opposite sides of the truck. We are sitting next to an elderly couple who look even more anxious than we do. They lived a life before the rapture. I couldn't imagine what it would be like to know how it was before and now be forced to live in this garbage dump we call a world. On the other side of the elderly couple, I see two girls of about our age, one with curly hair and one with straight hair. The pair have clearly been hardened by the wasteland and seem to be in top physical condition. I notice them take a glance at Ezra and I before their expressions turn sour. They start whispering to each other, and without warning one of them lunges at Ezra and tries to bite him in the leg. He kicks her off without much trouble and starts screaming,

"What the fuck is your problem?"

"You did this. It's all your fucking fault you murderer, I'm going to kill you I swear to God," she shouts back as guards come up on to the truck to restraint her.

The guard that had walked onto the truck slaps the woman across the face and shouts,

"Don't damage the cargo, or we will leave you tied up on the road!"

The girl recoils. Ezra and I meet eyes and try to non-verbally reconcile what has just happened. Then, in an instant, it clicks. The girls we overheard that night in the forest and the people who shot Ezra that fateful day in Omaha, our memories of both instances make the conclusion clear. Our pursuers, the ones who have caused so much pain, now lie right before us, just as helpless as we are.

*   *   *

August 11

So far, the trip has been unpleasant but uneventful. The two girls have stared at us with a burning hatred for almost the entire ride, but their restraints have kept them from being able to do anything. Each time they give me a death glare, I return it in full force. Let them know that I despise them just as much as they despise me. Still, I wish to know what we have done to gain their hatred, but it seems like I won't get to know now, as we aren't allowed to talk aboard the kidnapping express. We stop for the night at 11 PM and wake up at around 4 AM every morning, making us dead tired for the ride. Unfortunately, or fortunately depending on how you look at it, we still travel at a snail's pace because of all the debris that must be cleared from the road for the truck to pass. It's a heavy-duty truck, made for off-road environments, but it's far from its heyday now, and time has taken its toll. Regardless, the truck moves much faster than a person traveling by foot ever could. As of now, they have taken us down I-55 south. We entered Missouri at some point yesterday and have continued down the interstate since then. Even though I fear our destination, I hope it arrives soon.

With each passing moment we get farther and farther away from our goal, away from South Bend. We were only about five days away when they got us, but now… who knows if we'll ever be able to return. No, I can't allow myself to think like that. Somehow, we will make it out of this. Somehow, we will make it back to South Bend. I look at Ezra and make eye contact with him. I love him, and I am not going to let any harm come to him. No matter the cost.

*   *   *

The sun has just set, but on the horizon, I see something. It seems to be a walled town, but one that's full of electric lights. The whole journey here I figured that we would probably end up being slaves of some kind, but still, it didn't make any sense to me. Large towns can't exist because agriculture can't either. How can they keep us as slaves if we can't farm? Despite my concerns, what I see can't be denied: a relatively large settlement lies on the horizon. A while back I saw a sign that said "Entering Tennessee" so I know our approximate location. Even though I have been expecting this moment, the fact that it is here is truly terrifying.

Soon enough we arrive at a large wooden gate, with the word Providence painted across the top of it. The gates open, and our truck travels through it into its main square. The houses are all made of wood, and there seems to be around twenty of them in this area. From its size, I would estimate that it has a population of between 200 and 300 people. More surprising than any of that is that all the buildings here seem to have been built *after* the rapture, given the lack of modern construction conventions such as concrete. We come to a stop in the middle of the grassy square at the center of Providence. I hear the engine shut off and the two captors that have driven us here get out of the cabin. Two by two, they take us off the truck and start leading us towards the biggest house on the square. We are the third pair to be taken off the truck and luckily, it doesn't seem as if they are going to separate us now, which is one of my deeper fears about this place.

They lead us into the foyer of this large building before opening two double doors, bringing us into a wide open, empty room with an elevated stage in front of it. The other captives are scattered about the room, all facing the stage. Our captors do the same for us, shoving us to our knees with undue force. They leave us alone in this room as they head back to the truck to transport more prisoners. I consider trying to make an escape here, but considering my zip tied hands, I don't think I could get very far. The other captives look to be stoic, and none of them seem to be breaking down. This is just another day in the wasteland, I suppose.

After a few minutes, all the captives have been moved into this room. Our former pursuers, the two girls, are still glaring at us. I know that look in their eyes. If we gave them the chance, they would kill either of us in an instant. Suddenly, a booming voice echoes around the room. I turn to see a tall, muscular man stride towards the center of the stage. He has a long beard and cleanly cut hair, tan skin from long days in the sun, and strong arms from heavy manual labor. He has the body of a worker, but his voice and his charisma are that of a leader.

"I am sure you are all wondering why you have been brought to our lovely little town. Before any of your worries run astray, I will tell you that you have not been brought here to be eaten, brutalized, or harmed in any way shape or form. In fact, being brought here will be a benefit to you, as long as you follow the rules."

Based on the way that he speaks, the emphasis he puts on certain words, it is clear to me that he did public speaking before the Rapture or has done a lot of it ever since. He's certainly much older than the Rapture - I would guess in his late forties or early fifties.

"But first, let me introduce myself. My name is Tobias, but most folk around here just call me The Judge. I run Providence, and I have since around the time of its founding, soon after the Rapture. Now I'm sure you all are probably wondering; how can a town so large sustain itself? Well, that's where all of you come in. We bring in many workers to comb the land around us for all edible goods, and in exchange we provide you with housing and security from any raiders."

Putting on this facade of a nice guy while ordering us to be kidnapped and shipped away from everything we know into this unfamiliar town ... I can't stand him already.

"The only issue is that, in order to keep this last bastion of civilization running, we can't have our workers wandering off because they don't understand what we are trying to build here. To make sure that this doesn't happen, you were all brought in pairs. If while gathering or hunting outside of Providence, you decide that you want to forsake humanity and make a run for it, your partner will be executed. And trust me, I *never* want to have to do this, but sometimes sacrifices have to be made for the greater good. To enact this system, each of you has been given a bracelet with a number engraved upon it, with each pair sharing the same number. If you are seen without your bracelet, you must have an adequate excuse for why it has been broken and be carrying the damaged bracelet with you so a replacement can be made."

Slaves. Just as I thought. He's making us slaves, just with some extra flowery language to justify it.

"Still, I would never want any of you to think that we are simply abusing you for the good of Providence. After one year of working the land around this town, you will become a full citizen of Providence, as long as you display loyalty to our town. Once you are a full citizen, you are free to enjoy the luxuries we have to offer or leave and never turn back if that is what you so desire. And one more thing, we do not tolerate any violence among the workers. Once you enter the gates of Providence, the wasteland ends, and civilization begins. I hope that in one year's time, I will see all of you as full citizens of Providence," he states before turning and walking off the stage.

I'm not Ezra, but even I can sense math as bad as that. If the population of citizens in Providence keeps increasing like that, the number of workers needed to support that population would have to grow at an impossibly fast rate. If the workers are to have any food at all, there will at least need to be a 1:1 ratio of workers to citizens. If the citizens effectively double their population yearly, there is no way to sustain that population through the means Tobias just stated. To me, it seems likely that either all the workers die before reaching the one-year mark, most likely from starvation, or when a worker reaches the one-year mark, Tobias just says that they haven't proven their loyalty yet. Simply working our way out of this situation is not going to be an option. I'm sure Ezra knows as well as I that if we want to survive, we are going to have to make an escape.

The men who brought us in here are nowhere to be seen, but new guards come and escort us to our homes in Providence. One of them grabs my arm and yanks me to a standing position. I grunt a little from the force, and she gives me a look of disapproval and disdain in return. The cabins are only about a two-minute walk away from the entrance, which could be beneficial in terms of plotting our escape. Still, though, trying to get out the main gate would likely incite a hail of bullets from the patrols on the wall. The guards bring us to a wide-open field within the walls populated by about 10 cabins, each seemingly big enough for around fifteen people. That would likely put the population of providence at around 300 including both slaves and non-slaves. The idea of a rebellion might be feasible, but it would all depend on where the weapons are stored and how easily we could access them. I halt my mental process for a moment and decide to just absorb information for now and plot our escape later. I shouldn't let myself get attached to a particular plan only to find that it doesn't work given the introduction of a new factor.

The cabins are separated by gender, which I suppose makes sense as a pregnant worker is not nearly as useful. And thank god that means we aren't in the same cabin as those two girls, or it would be likely that we would wake up with slit throats. The cabin itself is plain, just wooden logs forming the walls with a plain gable roof atop it. The interior is dilapidated, with spiderwebs forming in the corners and the ground covered in dirt. The walls are lined with bunk beds with sheetless mattresses, although they appear to not be too nasty. Could be worse I suppose.

"Take a seat along the bunks, one person per mattress."

We do as he asks; I take the top bunk and Ezra takes the bottom. The mattress has some mildew on it, but certainly not the most disgusting I have seen. I turn my focus back to the man that is directing us. He seems to be the overseer of this operation. Looks like a real no-bullshit kind of guy; I don't want to try anything around him.

"So, here's how this is going to work. Every morning at 6 AM, the alarm will sound, waking all of you up. Following that it will exclaim a letter, A or B. On A days, the people on the bottom bunk will be responsible for leaving Providence in search of food. On B days, it's the same but for the top bunk people. To exit Providence, take a right when you leave your cabin and head straight until you reach the gate. This is also where you will be given the items that were confiscated from you. Providence will take fifty percent of all food you bring in to support job diversification within the town. The remainder of that food is to be split between you and your partner. If you are not hunting, line up outside your cabin by 6:30 AM. From there, you will be assigned a task for the day," the man sternly says.

This is going to be very difficult. Sharing fifty percent of one person's gains will not be able to sustain us for very long at all. The longer we wait, the weaker we become, making escape even harder.

"Now we get to the less pleasant parts. If you provide us with Sin contaminated food, the punishment is death for you and your partner, but know that we do test our food regardless, so it's not like you would even make an impact. Hiding food and not surrendering it to Providence is punishable by public whipping for you and your partner. Conspiring to escape is punishable by death for you and your partner. Fornication is punishable by public whipping for you and your partner. Not returning to Providence before sundown is punishable by death to your partner. Other actions may receive punishment at the Overseer's discretion. These rules are posted by the entrance to each cabin. Oh, and one more thing, if you catch anyone plotting an escape, and you tell me and provide proof, you will receive a month's worth of additional rations."

I knew that the stakes were going to be high, but to hear it put so explicitly causes my heart to race. Well, if inaction brings certain death and action only brings the possibility of it, I'll choose action any day.

"Tomorrow will be an A day, so those on the bottom be prepared to go out. Your supplies will be any hunting materials that you had prior to being brought to Providence. If you lack any supplies, we can provide you with a bow and ten arrows as well as a knife. In the free hours from 7 to 9 on Wednesdays, we have a class in Cabin One on the edible flora of the region. Welcome to civilization and good night to all of you."

What day is it? That's something Ezra and I have never bothered to keep track of. I have always kept the date, or at least tried my best but the day? It never seemed meaningful to me. I suppose this is what comes with living in "civilization." The overseer exits the cabin, leaving us all just staring at each other, most of us still not fully understanding the gravity of our situation. The cabin is full of all types of people, young and old, buff and skinny, tall and short. But the one similarity between all of them is the fear evident in their eyes.

As time passes, we start to snap out of it, turning to our respective bunkmates to discuss what has just happened. The first thing I do is give Ezra a long hug. I hadn't been able to touch him for days, so now that I finally can I'm going to make good use of it. Ezra returns the hug and buries his face into my shoulder. I've thought this before, I know, but once we are out of here, I'm going to tell him how I feel. My life is far too short to waste by hiding this from him. After a few moments, we recede from each other's embrace. I know that Ezra is smart enough to realize all the things that I have during the man's speech, so I simply tell him,

"We are going to get out of this, I promise."

He looks into my eyes and responds, "I know."

Chapter 12- Ezra

August 12

Just like the overseer said it would, the alarm wakes me up with the loud exclamation that today is an A day. I grab my dirty jeans and shirt, which I hadn't been able to wash or change for the past few days for obvious reasons. I pull my legs over the side of the bed and put on my clothes, bearing their musty smell. The layer of dirt and sweat that has built itself up upon my skin makes me feel absolutely disgusting, but until I find a river, there's not much I can do about it. I look back up at the bunk and see Quinn sit up and look at me getting ready to go. I wave him back to sleep since he still has thirty minutes before he needs to turn the cog, he's responsible for in this wonderful machine they call civilization. The other people in the bottom bunks are getting ready just as I am and are clearly just as anxious too. I was the first to leave my cabin and start following the directions that the overseer gave me last night. As I walk, I feel a pit of anxiety growing in my stomach about the coming hours. Being left out in the open with one of those girls who has pursued Quinn and me for hundreds of miles makes me more than just apprehensive. And worse, if she manages to find and kill me out there, Quinn will share the same fate. Even though I am tired, I feel grateful that it's early, as the weather is bearable without the sun. However, this will not be the case for long, so either I have to find a shaded area, or find some mud to cover myself in to avoid a sunburn.

As I reach the crowded gate, my mind shifts away from thoughts of the weather. There are three parallel rows of workers facing the gate. Considering that my cabin is in the last row, I figure that this is probably where I should stand. Over the next five or so minutes, more workers begin to congregate around the gate. Soon enough it seems that there are around 150 people standing here waiting for orders. Finally, the man at the front of the gate starts calling numbers. I look down at mine to remind myself what it is: 3762-2. So far, I see no sign of either of the two girls, but I know that unless they tried something stupid, at least one of them will be here. I can't see super well because I am in the back, but from here it looks like each person being called is being handed their bag before being escorted out of the gate. I wonder if they took my math textbook away. It's a stupid thought; Algebra II certainly won't help me here, but that textbook has been with me a while and I would be deeply saddened by its absence.

After about three minutes I hear my number being called by the man's deep and gruff voice. I rush over and turn my wrist to reveal my number. Another man standing by the announcer picks up my bag from the row lined up against the wall and slams it into my chest. He tells me to head south and be back before sunset before pointing me towards the open gate. The girl still hasn't left Providence yet, so I figure that I should try to get a head start on her before taking inventory of what tools and weapons I possess. But even if I can evade her today, there's no assurance about the next time. In truth, this situation just isn't going to be sustainable. Considering how long the girls tracked us, they will stop at nothing until we are in the grave.

I resolve to formulate a plan with Quinn when I return. For today, my goal is simply to find something to eat.

I figure that based on the volume of people being sent out to hunt, it's probably in my best interest to try to put as much distance between me and Providence as I can. Hunting a Sinless creature is hard enough, but if seventy-five hunters are doing it at the same time, it becomes nigh impossible. As I walk, I think about Providence, mainly about the horrid injustice of its existence. Even knowing that I am part of the same species as the people that are perpetuating such wrongdoing weighs me down heavily. If the cost of civilization is kidnapping people and forcing them to work or have their loved ones executed, I don't want it. Despite this, I wouldn't say I feel misanthropic, just disgusted at what Sin has brought us to. I can't tell if it's just the rage speaking, but at that moment, I am filled with a desire to burn the whole city down.

I stop for a moment to look at some seemingly edible berries growing at the base of a large oak tree. I pluck one of the berries from its stem, holding it between my index finger and my thumb. I'm not Quinn, so I can't name exactly what this berry is, but I feel like I have seen Quinn bring me something that looked like this, so as long as it doesn't have Sin, I figure I might just eat these right now to avoid the tax Providence would exact if I were to bring them back. I'm far enough now that I think I have time to dig through my bag to see what exactly they have taken and what exactly is left. The Algebra II textbook is missing, which I suppose makes sense since it's not needed for hunting. My rifle is missing too, but my bow does seem to be in here, although it has been taken apart so it could fit within the bag. Oddly enough there is a new addition to the contents of the bag in the form of a group of zip ties. I bet there is a hefty reward for bringing in a pair of new slaves, although I doubt that too many people pass through here. Finally, I notice that my pistol and my hunting knife are both still present. Other miscellaneous items such as pots and utensils appear to be missing as well, but all in all, it's not too bad. At the bottom of the back, I notice something with a golden lining, which, as I pull it out, reveals itself to be the *Guild of Oleander*. For some reason they let me keep it, which I make a mental note to take advantage of. I snatch the hunting knife and prick my finger after slicing open the berry, as I have done hundreds of times before. The droplet of blood falls on to the sweet flesh, and quickly begins to boil and bubble. I've seen this happen so many times before, yet oddly enough I've never seen what it's like when a human eats a Sin-ridden food.

My thought process is rudely interrupted when out of the corner of my eye, I spot it. Movement that can only belong to a human, and if there's a human this close to me, there's only one probable solution. There is a chance that this is some random raider but given how those girls had chased us across the country, I am confident in the identity of my attacker. I duck behind the tree in front of me just as a bullet slams into the ground where I once was. The boom of the gunshot rolls across the woods, which to the other slaves, probably just seems to be the sign of a hunt gone right. To me, however, this gunshot represents a choice: either I can kill her now or I can try to incapacitate her somehow. Normally this choice would be a no-brainer. She's trying to kill me, and right now, both Quinn's life and my own are on the line. I can take whatever force is necessary to ensure our safety. One thing gnaws at me though, which is that if I kill her, I kill her sister too. As it is now, I have no clue if this one is the driving force behind our pursuit, and the other was merely dragged along for the ride. I was willing to kill both when I thought they were hunting me, but today I would be killing a woman who was simply sitting in her cabin doing no harm. I won't die today, that's for certain. I think about the other girl, about her potential public execution, about the fear and anger she would experience in that moment. Against my better instincts, I decide that unless I absolutely must kill her, I'm going to take her in.

About a hundred feet ahead of me there is a large boulder. If I can make it there without being struck by one of her bullets, I could easily ambush her as she pursues me. The hard part about this plan is managing to get there unscathed. By now she's probably reloaded the rifle and has it trained on the oak tree behind me. This area is very heavily wooded, which should give me the advantage I need to make it to the boulder. After a few more seconds of thinking in this heated silence, I come up with a plan. I take my pistol and zip ties out of the bag and then chuck it out of the tree's cover. Just as I suspected, the throwing of the bag is quickly followed by a loud crack, meaning that she fired at the first sign of movement regardless of what it was. I sprint from behind cover as fast as I can, turning my arm and firing suppressing shots in her general direction as I run. The recoil of the weapon with each bullet fired is an unwelcome reminder of the power I hold in my hand, and the weight of the choice I will have to make in the coming moments.

I can't stop running and hide behind a tree, because if I do, she just has to train her weapon on it and wait for me to move. Instead, I use the trees as cover while staying mobile, keeping her guessing as to my position until I pop out into an opening between trees, firing shots back at her to keep her from being able to accurately aim when I do. My arm aches from the wound that very rifle had inflicted upon me a month ago. Even after this time, I'm by no means healed and if I keep up this rigorous activity, I will probably tear the stitching Quinn had so carefully put in place.

The boulder is fast approaching, probably only about 20 or 30 feet away. Another bullet slams into the dirt next to my foot. The seconds seem to stretch into eternity as the boulder nears, but after avoiding one more blast of her rifle, I make it behind the stone wall. I take a few deep breaths while I sit behind the safety of the stone shield. My shoulder begins to throb even harder. I have to end this now, no matter the cost. Based on where I saw the bullets coming from, I anticipate that she will probably come around the left side of the boulder, but I keep my pistol pointed towards the right side just in case. I don't want to kill her, but if she comes around the other way, I will have no choice. My heart is pounding as I wait, adrenaline keeping the fear from seeping into my bones. After what feels like an eternity, I finally hear the footsteps of someone sprinting towards the boulder's left side.

I hold my pistol in my right hand, with a fist clenched in my left. I will try to hit her over the head with the butt of my pistol, and what happens to her after that will be up to whatever god she believes in. She rounds the corner, her face bursting with surprise as she identifies my attack. My weapon arcs towards her head, but she manages to bring her arms up to block right before the hard metal makes contact with her skull. With my off-hand, I go for a straight punch to the gut. She is still recoiling from the force of the first impact as my fist connects with her stomach. I throw all my weight behind it, trying to knock her to the floor. She may be very muscular, and I may be injured, but if I can turn this into a wrestling match, my superior size should allow me to win. I see her lose her balance, so I dive forward to try to land on top of her. However, just as I land, she swings her arm and slices my leg with a hunting knife faster than I could even process her attack. The shooting pain in my leg gives her the opportunity to shove me off before going for a lethal blow to the throat. I manage to roll out of her attack, leaving her knife embedded in the ground. I make one final dive at her, pushing her back on the ground before she has a chance to recover her knife.

I pin both of her hands to the ground, but that doesn't stop her from thrashing with an intense vigor. Looking at her face, I see nothing, but pure, unadulterated loathing spread across every visible feature. I slam my forehead into her nose to try to disorient her. She recoils for a moment, pausing her thrashing and giving me an opportunity to roll her onto her back before tying two zip ties firmly around her arms. As I do, she screams the most primal, rage-filled scream I have ever heard, echoing across the forest around us. I take off her backpack and search her pockets to ensure that she doesn't have any tricks up her sleeve to get out of this. While I have her here, I figure that it's finally time to get some answers.

"Why have you chased us half-way across the country?" I ask sternly.

"To kill you," she responds in a quiet monotone.

"Why do you want to kill me?"

"You killed my father."

The moment that she says that I know who she must be talking about. The raider that I shot back in the village in Colorado. I always assumed that those raiders thought we were dead, but clearly, this shows me that they didn't. As everything falls into place, my soul feels like it's melting. The anguish, the hate, the malice that lives in this person is something that I have cultivated. I did what I must to save Quinn, but seeing the horrific damage it has caused brings me to the edge of a breakdown. In that moment, the slightest bit of doubt about all I have done begins to creep into place. I did what was right, but if this monster of pure vengeance and hatred is what resulted from it, how could I possibly have been justified?

"I did what I had to in self-defense. While in other circumstances I would be alright with leaving this broken world, I'm afraid I just can't let you kill me."

"Spare me the lies. Regardless of what you say, I will kill you. I will hunt you until your heart stops beating. Whether it takes a day, a year, or a decade, I will not rest until your corpse lies lifeless on the floor."

She clearly has some false idea of what happened, but regardless, the kind of hate that brews in her is not easily cooled. Even if she were somehow convinced of the true circumstances of her father's death, would that even mean anything? If what she says is true, I should just kill her now. If she will never stop hunting Quinn and me, that means I should just end her here. Still, what kind of person would I be if I murdered a helpless woman while she is completely at my mercy? In that case, would I be just as vile as she thinks

I am now? Would I be any better than the mongrels who kidnapped all these people and brought them here?

I sit there with a knife in my hand. The surroundings are quiet, with only a few bugs and birds chirping in the distance. This world is cruel, far too cruel. If I must be cruel if I want to survive, then I refuse to survive. I care about Quinn more than anything else, that's a constant. But after all I have seen, all I have done, can I really let myself be all the evil I have witnessed? How could I possibly take the role of executioner into my own hands? I stand up and pull the woman to her feet. She grunts softly as I lift her, but otherwise she has stayed silent since she made her last threats. I figure I should just take her back to Providence and they can handle her. They wouldn't want their slaves killing each other so I figure that they will take action. I collect the materials I had discarded during my escape from this woman. My backpack now has a bullet hole through it, but luckily it didn't seem to damage any of the interior components.

I contemplate asking this woman her name but realize that it would be a fruitless endeavor before I even attempt it. It's still morning, meaning despite the new strain on my shoulder and the cut on my leg I should continue searching for food after I bring her in. I'm surprised that she isn't putting up much of a fight as I escort her. She must just think that she should wait for a better time to try and take me out. As I walk, the pain in my shoulder becomes harder to ignore. I glance down at my shoulder and luckily, it doesn't seem as if the wound has reopened. In the future, I will have to be more careful until I'm back at one hundred percent.

Soon enough, Providence comes back into view. The guard in front of the main gate to Providence gives us a strange look as we approach, although judging from the fact that he's keeping his weapon lowered, he doesn't seem to be threatened. Once we come within speaking distance, he calls out to me,

"What are you doing with that woman there?"

"She's another worker at Providence. She tried to kill me. I believe that she has a vendetta against me and won't stop until she achieves it."

"And what do you say, woman?"

"I have no idea what he's talking about."

"Look, I even have the slashes to prove it," I say before exposing the wound that she had carved into my leg.

"Honestly, I don't give a shit what happened between you two, but we can't have workers killing each other. I'm editing the contingency log. If either of you two don't come home, the other, as well as both corresponding partners will be executed. Now, show me your numbers."

I reach out my wrist to reveal the number carved into the bracelet. This is a good solution. It should keep either of them from harming us at least until we get out of Providence. The woman doesn't seem to be reaching out her wrist, so I grab her arm and start pushing it out for her. She resists me, but I have strength on my side, making my venture successful.

"The 3762 and 3740 pairs are now joined. Make sure to pass it down," the guard calls to his companion a way down the wall.

"Thank you," I say to the guard before letting the woman go and turning to retreat into the forest.

"Don't forget, you have to be back before sundown."

I nod and continue pressing on towards finding some food. The second I let the woman go, she darts away in the other direction. I guess she just couldn't bear to look at me a moment longer. Though I suppose, being fair to her, that isn't too strange given what I've done. Thinking about it now, if I had any way of finding the person that killed Melchior, I probably would have followed a path similar to hers. The weight of my actions hangs heavily over me as I walk. If I just hadn't pushed Quinn to run into the village, that woman's father would still be alive, we never would have learned about Ichthys, and neither of our pairs would be stuck as slaves in an unfamiliar land. But then again, if we never went into the village on that fateful day, those that we saved would be six feet under. For a moment I wonder whether that would have been better for them, given how shitty this world is. I expel that thought from my mind. They wanted to live. I can't tell them that their life isn't worth living.

The rest of the day passes without trouble. I only see one other worker in passing for the entirety of the day, but otherwise I remained unbothered. I managed to hunt two Sin-less rabbits today which was certainly a victory, but the fact I must surrender one of them fills me with anger. I arrive back at Providence a half hour early to ensure that I make it back in time. I return through the gates and wander over to a desk where I mark off my findings of the day and yield what I must. Once that is complete, I take what food I have and walk through the seemingly endless rows of cabins back towards the one where we reside. As I look around at the towers of wood and stone surrounding me, I can't help but feel that we are going to be here for a long, long time.

Chapter 13- Quinn

August 12

I lay in my bunk as Ezra walks in the cabin door, rabbit in tow. I thank the gods of chance for his luck. I couldn't imagine what would happen if I wasn't able to eat today. Still, when I look at him, there is a somberness to his face I wouldn't have expected given his relative success. As he approaches, he asks:

"Come on, let's go find a place to cook this. Then, I have something important to share with you."

I follow him out of the cabin door and into the common square, where many cooking fires burn. We find a somewhat secluded spot and take a seat. Ezra had grabbed some of the communal firewood on the way over, so he begins constructing the fire as he explains the events of today.

I almost can't believe what he says. To think that those girls had tracked us all the way from Colorado. I suppose if they went through the Ichthys facility, they might have found our final destination, and from there they just had to follow the route. Nonetheless, the fact that they have found us on three separate occasions is mind boggling to me. And this new rule that they are imposing, what if one of the sisters independently tries to run away or something, then Ezra and I are just fucked? He said that this was a good solution to keep them from killing us, but to me this seems like another way for us to get killed. I wouldn't say it to Ezra, but I think he should have just killed her while she was in the forest. I don't think that I would have done it, but after my actions in Omaha, I can't be so sure.

I look around the open square and see dozens of pairs of dirty, hopeless humans cooking and eating whatever scraps they could manage. Many of them are completely emaciated, not even strong enough to stand up. I imagine that Providence officials don't even force them to go out looking for food, they just let them lie and stare at the sky, waiting for their inevitable deaths. These are only a small portion of those laid out before me. Most are thin to be sure, but still capable of functioning. They speak with each other as they eat, but their voices are weak and defeated. In the center of the square lies the blood-stained executioner's block, a grim reminder to all who eat here of the circumstances of our servitude. This square has the facade of a feast: the roaring fires, the cooking food, the loving company, but really, it was more like a hall of the living dead.

In spite of all of this, I can't find it in me to hate the people who run this place, as evil as it is. Ever since Omaha, the lines between good and bad people have become a lot more blurred for me. People generally do things for one of two reasons: circumstances or genetics. Neither of these are under our control. This isn't just me trying to excuse my own actions, it's just that those actions, which were undoubtedly wrong, helped me understand that people follow that path because it seems like the only one to them. It's bullshit to me that some softie who never lived in the apocalypse gets to be a 'good person' because they never killed anyone. I'd bet that if anyone were in my shoes, they would do exactly what I have, if not worse. Right and wrong are an illusion, all that matters are genetics and circumstances. Considering this epiphany, I've decided to renounce hatred, justice, and righteous punishment. It will be without any hatred, without any justice, and without any sense of righteous punishment that I will tear this place to the ground.

"Quinn, are you alright?"

"Yeah, sorry, I got a little distracted there."

I look at the cooked rabbit that Ezra is offering me. I accept it eagerly, my hunger on clear display. The plain, unseasoned rabbit tasted like the finest delicacy after days of eating almost nothing. In mere moments, Ezra and I manage to devour the entire animal. Both of us are still left completely unsatisfied, which is even worse since today was a good day in terms of hunting. As we sit opposing the now smothered fire, Ezra asks,

"So, what have you done today? What have you learned of the interior of Providence?"

"They had my group act as janitors for the mess hall. I think it's probably because we're the least starved, meaning we're probably the only workers who can be around their abundant food without being too tempted to steal any. But anyway, the job consisted of sweeping, mopping, and otherwise cleaning the mess hall and kitchen between jobs. The citizens of Providence each get a plate with different foods collected by the workers, normally some type of berry with some type of meat, maybe even some mushrooms if they're lucky. It's just like they say it is, civilization built off the back of barbarism."

"Did you notice any weaknesses or flaws in anything you saw?"

"Well, the major weakness that I've seen is that all the buildings around here are made of wood. We couldn't just set the cabins on fire because they aren't connected to the living and working quarters of the citizens, but if we got into the city center with some sort of fire starter, we might have a chance of being able to take this place out and escape in the process."

"That might work, but it's going to need some prep and a lot of luck. We need to make sure we don't get tunnel vision and keep our options open. Did you learn anything more about Providence?"

"They are happy," I mutter loudly enough for Ezra to hear.

"What?"

"The people. When you see them in the mess hall you will understand. On their faces it's clear, the levity, the joy, the fulfillment. It's all there. And it's our duty to take it from them. Any happiness that they have was never theirs to begin with, it was just stolen from the tortured souls that they have kidnapped and forced to work for them."

Our conversation goes silent, and I go back to my observations of the surrounding people. Today, despite everything that I see and everything that has happened, I'm hopeful. Hopeful that I can get out of this place and bring it down with me.

* * *

August 13

The morning alarm hits like a truck. I see that below me Ezra is already awake, even though he doesn't have to be for another thirty minutes. In his hands he holds the *Guild of*

Oleander, open to what looks like the center of the book. Even though I know it would be better for him if he would have just gone to sleep, seeing that book bring him some measure of peace warms my heart. I put on my dirty clothes and hop out of bed. Taking a sniff of my shirt, I resolve that I should probably try to wash these at some point today.

I give Ezra a small wave as I stroll out of the cabin and towards the gate. Even if it's just for a while, the idea of leaving Providence makes my heart pound with excitement. After arriving at the gate, I wait for my number to be called with the other workers. The man in line next to me turns and reaches out his hand.

"Name's Finn. I'm from your cabin."

I shake his hand before saying, "Nice to meet you. Name's Quinn"

"I figured if we are going to be living together, we ought to know each other's names. Plus, it wouldn't be too bad to have a friend or two in this place."

A friend isn't exactly what I'm looking for here, but nonetheless I nod. His friendliness is appreciated, but I can't let myself get attached to anyone. My only obligation is to Ezra. This is the way it has to be. My number echoes through the air; without hesitation, I snatch my dearly missed bag and run out the gate with clear urgency, giving Finn a faint wave as I do. While I'm not looking for a friend, I'm not looking for an enemy either. As soon as the walls of Providence fade from view, something dawns on me. I'm going to have to hunt. There's just no way around it. Now that Ezra and I can't split up our tasks, it means that we each must hunt and gather if we want to maximize our food intake. I stop for a minute to take stock of my weapons and resources.

"Stop," a woman's voice yells from behind me.

I try to get hold of my pistol but realize if she already has a weapon pointed at me, I'm as good as gone. I turn my head and unsurprisingly, it's one of the two sisters that have been chasing us. Her weapon isn't drawn, but I can see her keeping her hand at her side, holding the grip of a pistol.

"I thought we weren't allowed to kill each other," I reply matter-of-factly.

"That's right, and I'm here to ensure that you don't end up getting killed or running away, because I quite like being alive and so does my sister. As much as I would like to shoot you in the head for being a piece of scum and accomplice in my father's murder, I care much more that my sister lives. My name's Kayla, and my sister's name is Astrid by the way."

"My name's-"

"Shut up, I don't care what your name is. I only told you mine to remind you that I am a person, one that has suffered because of you. I want you to feel just a fraction of the pain that you have caused me," she says, the loathing evident in her voice.

"Well, us staying together this whole time probably won't work if we want to get an adequate amount of food."

"Fine, but don't get too far away from me, and I want you to check in with me at this location at least every hour."

That deal certainly sounds annoying, but if it keeps her from my throat, it'll be worth it.

"Alright, I'll try that for now."

I stride away, and once out of sight realize how tense that encounter made me. That woman is the enemy. She made me do what I did in Omaha. But she only "made" me do that because we "made" her come after us by killing her father who "made" us kill him. It's a never-ending chain that started with the dawn of humanity and was only exacerbated by the apocalypse. Despite all the hate I want to harbor for her, I go back to what I was thinking earlier. It's all genetics and circumstances. No one is deserving of punishment because we are all just victims of our own birth.

As I walk, I see a few edible plants, but also many that I am unable to identify. I take the ones that I can and resolve to go to that class Providence offers on Wednesdays. About thirty feet in front of me I notice something moving. Upon closer inspection I determine that it is a rabbit that has been caught in a snare trap. I see it wriggle and flail, the desperation evident in its eyes. This is clearly someone else's quarry, but in Providence, the rule is always finders keepers. Without much hesitation, I reach up and snap the rabbit's neck. It lets out a squeal as it dies, launching another blow against my heart. I release the rabbit from the snare and lay it on the ground so I can test it for Sin. After following Ezra's recommended procedure and taking off a patch of skin, I let a droplet of my blood fall onto its bare flesh. The blood starts to turn a pinkish color and bubble, clearly indicating that this rabbit has Sin.

I grab the rabbit and decide to get away from the snare in case its owner comes looking for it. Quickly, as I do not have much time, I use my hands to dig a small hole in the ground. I lay the rabbit down into it before covering it with dirt once more. I have taken its life for naught, so I may as well give it what little respect that I can. I run back to the meeting spot with Kayla to avoid her ire. I reach it before her and wait for her appearance. I see her walking towards me from the west and give her a little wave to make sure she can see me. She nods to me as a way of acknowledging my presence before turning around. All the better for her if she doesn't have to speak to me, I guess.

After walking for about thirty seconds, I notice a minute bit of movement out of the corner of my eye. Turning my head, I see that it is the flash of the tip of an antler as its owner passes behind me. Rifle in hand, I crouch down and point my weapon at where I suspect the heart of the now grazing deer would be.

Bang.

The deer moves just as I shoot, causing my bullet to hit it in a non-vital area. As I chase the fleeing deer, I reload the next bullet into the weapon's chamber. Unfortunately, I find it much too difficult to line up a shot at this distance given the many trees between me and my target.

The deer falls over dead. I look for the source of the shot to see Kayla striding towards her prize. I make my way over to the deer just as Kayla pricks her finger to test it for Sin.

"I got the first shot, so we should split it," I say as I approach.

She turns her head and gives me a death stare. Splitting it would be common courtesy for any two people who are amicable. Unfortunately, Kayla and I are not so. Still, I'm sure that she recognizes that for her and Kayla to live, Ezra and I must live. For that to occur, both of us need to eat.

"Fine, but just this once. I need your help to carry it back into Providence anyways."

And carry it back into Providence we do. Judging off the gazes of the guards that we pass by it seems like it's relatively unusual for such a large animal to be caught and to be Sinless. Doesn't bother me though. I'm not complaining. After we split up the remainder of the deer once Providence takes its share, I'm still left with a hearty sum of meat. I decided to salt it and turn it into jerky for longevity. Surprisingly, Providence provides me salt at no cost. That must be the one of the "luxuries of civilization" that I have heard oh so much about.

The rest of the day passes quickly. After I'm done salting most of the meat, I just wait in the empty cabin to try to get away from the afternoon sun. Soon enough, Ezra comes back from his daily task, and I inform him about my escapades of the day. His day seemed to be boring, just helping to construct a new residential building in the northern part of the town. While we are talking, a bell rings that summons all of us to the common square outside of the worker cabins. In the center of the square lies a stage. It is generally where the public executions are done, but those do not necessitate the summoning of everyone, normally just the cabin mates and anyone who happens to be in the square at that time. On the stage is the Judge and two restrained people, who I infer to be workers, as well as three armed guards.

"Greetings, workers of Providence," the voice of the Judge booms from his megaphone.

It's faint, especially given the hum of the crowd and the Judge's loud speech, but the two workers are clearly whimpering, although I'm not sure if it's in pain or fear, or both.

"We here in Providence are all one big community, I'm sure that you know that. What we have within these walls is *truly* special. You could travel for hundreds, maybe even thousands of miles before you found any settlement as advanced as ours. This means that every inhabitant of this great town, whether they be worker or citizen, must toil together to ensure our continued prosperity."

I can see where this is going, and I don't like it. Not one bit.

"I know that some of you workers would rather not be here. Really, I understand. I was brought here against my will some sixteen odd years ago, right around when Providence was founded. But I worked hard, rose through the ranks, and now have one of the best lives in the wasteland."

He grabs one of the workers on the stage by the collar and lifts him up from his knees. Now that I can fully see his face, I realize that he doesn't appear to be older than fourteen. I grit my teeth in anger, but it is quickly replaced with pity. Pity that humanity was born into such circumstances that made us do such horrible things.

"Some of us have rejected this imperative, instead choosing to try to murder innocent men, women, and children in a foolish bid to avoid responsibility. This man is one of those fools. He tried to pour Sin-laced blood all over today's lunch supply at the dining hall. The school children coming in on their lunch break would have been the first and only ones to be melted by this vile plot. Luckily, he was noticed before he could finish his task. I am here today to show you that acts like these cannot go unpunished!"

He draws a bowie knife and stabs it through the boy's forearm. He tries to scream out in pain, but his gag muffles it to a mere whimper.

"As all of you know, Providence functions off a basis of responsibility for oneself and one's partner. This man has violated that responsibility."

He struts over to the boy's partner, a woman who seems to be much older, likely his mother. He lifts her up and slices his knife across her throat. She falls to the floor gurgling in her own blood. The boy was too busy trying to hold the gaping wound in his arm, but he notices his mother fall to the floor and releases another muffled cry of agony. The Judge returns to him and gives two slashes across his cheeks before turning back to the audience.

"Believe me, I get no pleasure from doing this. It is simply what must be done for the sake of the whole town. To make sure you all understand the consequences of tarnishing the contract we have established here at Providence, I'm going to leave this boy chained here until he expires. Thank you all for your time, goodnight."

The Judge walks off, escorted by armed guards. I am now more certain than ever in my conviction to eviscerate this pitiful "civilization.".

Chapter 14 - Ezra

September 1

The sticks on the forest floor make a satisfying crunch as Astrid and I walk upon them. I look up into her cold face, which is staring straight ahead. She hasn't said a word to me beyond what was necessary the whole time we have been walking together. If the pact that we have with Providence were to end now, there is no doubt that she would bring a knife to my throat without a second thought. Providence is keeping me alive. That's a funny thought. The morning sun hangs low in the sky and golden rays shine through the gaps in the canopy, giving me a wonderfully beautiful view of the forest. It would be quite peaceful if the circumstances were anything else.

When we reach the spot where we usually split up, I figure that we might have better luck if we go a little bit farther away from Providence. Astrid isn't pleased by the suggestion, but that's probably just because it's coming from me. We walk for about seven minutes longer before we happen across an anomaly. Straight across from us we see a road, and next to that road is a decaying, but still standing gas station.

"We should probably go in there, right?" I ask. "There could be some canned goods or otherwise useful materials."

"Yes, but be armed in case some roving bandits have decided to make it their home for the day."

We draw our weapons and stalk towards the gas station. There are a few letters on the front of the station that used to form a sign, but most of them are missing, leaving the word lost to time. We stay low and peer through the smashed window of the gas station. The shelves appear to be cleared and the room looks uninhabited. We look at the glass door of the station, but it's covered with so many vines and so much foliage that trying to enter through it would be more trouble than it's worth.

I carefully climb through the window opening, making sure to avoid the shattered glass at its rim. Astrid, however, does not seem to be so careful about avoiding the glass. Fortunately, just as she is about to scrape her leg against the sharp glass, I manage to warn her of the danger. She gives me the evil-eye but adjusts her actions accordingly. As we walk around the store, we are only greeted by more vacant shelves. I go up to where the register is, pretending that I was some pre-Sin shopper, here to buy all that I need in order to survive. My fantasy unravels the moment I arrive at the rusted, smashed open hunk of metal that used to be a cash register. Just as I am about to turn around, I notice something lodged in a little nook behind the employee's desk. I slide over the checkout desk and pull out this orange box from its semi-hidden spot.

Upon seeing what it is, my eyes glaze over in a cool excitement. A ten pack of disposable lighters. Lighter fluid means the ability to start an easy fire that doesn't require me to sit still for a minute. An easy fire and a wooden settlement generally do not go very well together. I can't let Astrid figure out the plan that is beginning to mentally take shape, so I throw the lighters in my bag before she can notice. I have no clue how I'm going to be able to smuggle the lighters into Providence given that they search us on re-entry, but I'm sure that Quinn and I can come up with a way once I tell him about them tonight. My frenzy of brainstorming is interrupted when I hear Astrid call,

"There's nothing here, let's go."

"Alright," I yell across the store.

I walk back towards the smashed window, unable to ignore the figurative weight of the lighters in my bag. I hop back out the window without a hitch, and Astrid follows suit. Astrid turns and keeps walking past the gas station without even saying a word to me, but I follow her regardless. For a long time, I contemplate saying something to her, trying to apologize for the hurt that I have caused her. But each time I come up with something to say, it all comes out wrong. The fact is that I'm the one that caused her to suffer. There isn't any getting around that. When I pulled that trigger, I irreversibly turned this person's life for the worse. Logically, I wouldn't say I regret what I have done, as I'm glad to have saved those three villagers, but the weight that my actions hold on my heart grows steadier each day. That means that not only do I recognize the unimaginable pain I have caused to this person, but would I be willing to do it again? What kind of person does that make me?

I just wish I could make her see from my perspective, get her to understand why I did what I did, but her mind is already too closed about us being evil and deserving of death. Maybe I am deserving of death, given the things I have done, the things I was willing to do, the things I *am* willing to do. But even if I do deserve to die, I can't until Providence is nothing but rubble. There's got to be some good in that, right? I shake my head and shut out these thoughts. I'm just going to say something to her and hope that this doesn't make things any worse.

"Astrid, I know that, to you, I am beyond redemption. But truly, I did not want to harm your father in any way. It was just the circumstances of this world that forced me to take action. And I realize that saying any of this doesn't take the pain away from what I have done. I am human, and I am not malicious, just trying to survive in this shitty world. All I ask is that you keep this in mind before you make the decision to kill me."

Right when I started speaking Astrid stopped in her tracks before turning and looking at me. As I speak, I can feel the burn of her hateful stare, making me just want to halt in the middle of my speech. But I power through it, leaving her still staring at me, only this time in complete silence save for the sound of the wind rustling through the trees. Without dignifying me with a response, Astrid turns back around and continues her walk. I try to follow her, but she turns and waves her finger no in response. I guess that means that it's time to split up then. So off on my own path I go, with a feeling of defeat looming over me. I really have no clue what to do about Astrid. It doesn't seem like she will ever renounce her hatred of us, nor stop hunting us down. I shouldn't really expect anything more than this though. If someone had killed Quinn, I don't know that there is anything that could convince me to abandon my vengeance against them. No, something must be done, I don't know what, but something must be done. With these thoughts floating through my head, I march away from Astrid in search of more life to destroy for my own survival.

*　*　*

There are no public executions today, which manages to make the ambience of the common area slightly less depressing. Quinn looks down at his meager helping of roots and leaves with a despairing look. Today had not brought great gains, and we lacked anything stored to eat, so edible roots it was. In the days before we arrived here at Providence, I would have been alarmed by a look such as the one Quinn holds now, but after my three-week tenure in this hell hole, I've realized that looks such as these are the norm. Still, I haven't yet told Quinn about my real find of the day, so hopefully that will be able to cheer him up even a little. I lean in close before saying, "I think I have the beginnings of a plan to tear this place down."

Quinn stops eating and looks at me intently. This is the phrase he has been waiting for since we got here.

To ensure that my plan is not overheard, I lean into Quinn and whisper, "I found a ten pack of lighters, tested each one of them and they are all working. That amount of lighter fluid might be enough to start a major fire in the main hall of Providence. If this fire then becomes visible to the workers, I'm sure that many of them will see it as their chance to escape and then run. In the panic, we kill the Judge. Hopefully, the guards will have to either put out the fire or stop the runaways, but in either case Providence falls."

"That sounds like a plan with a bunch of opportunities for failure and only one for success. I'm in. From how I'm looking at it, the difficulties we face now are what we will use to kindle the fire, how we will get the lighters into Providence, how we will get into the building to light the fire, and how we will disable their sprinkler system."

"Sprinkler system?"

"It's a more rudimentary version of the ones that they had back in the days before Sin. There are multiple large water tanks on top of the main building that holds the mess hall and most of the residential quarters. If they are activated at the top, they release water throughout the whole building below, which would smother our plans for a fire."

"That's troublesome, but I'm sure that we can figure our way around it. As for the tinder, I had already started thinking about that. Some of the other people in our cabin bring in fiber from the outside to pad their beds with. If it's common, I bet that we could get away with doing it ourselves."

Imagining this town in flames brings me primal joy, even though I recognize the pain and death that such an action will bring. I can't let myself think like that. Destroying this place will not be an indulgence but a necessity.

"As for smuggling in the lighters, we could try hiding them within the meats that we bring into Providence. They sometimes search all over our clothes, but they wouldn't think to look inside of the food we bring. We should smuggle them separately though, just in case they decide to commandeer extra food like they sometimes do."

"But wouldn't they find the lighter if they decided to take extra food?" I ask.

"They would, but by that point it would already be in the kitchen and have no connection to us."

"That doesn't mean that the Judge wouldn't do whatever he could to figure out who is smuggling."

"But he would fail. No one knows that we are smuggling, so no one would snitch."

"Still, he might hurt other people."

"Then don't let them find the lighter."

I nod, unhappy with that answer, but I'm cognizant of the fact it's our only way.

"So, we need to wait until we get assigned somewhere in the main hall that could let us access the sprinkler system, wait until we have enough tinder, and wait until we find a way into the main hall at night?" I say.

"It is a lot of waiting, but it's better than just waiting to die like almost everyone else around here is doing."

There is still one question that we both have left unanswered. What are we going to do about Astrid and Kayla? We could just leave them, but then they might chase after us. We could try to help them escape after we start the fire in hopes they will understand that we are not the villains they think we are. I know that Quinn thinks that we should kill the both of them to protect ourselves, but after seeing Astrid for the person she is and not just a nameless face, I know this is not an option. Both Quinn and I know we can't decide now, so we choose not to bring it up.

The rest of the night goes by quickly. By the time I climb into my hard and uncomfortable bed, the rush of joy that comes with the prospect of Providence's downfall has all but faded. All I am left with is dread of the toil and pain that tomorrow will bring.

* * *

September 4

I wake up to the sound of the second alarm calling me to do more work on Providence's behalf. I drudge through the processes of getting up and stumble towards the assignment yard. I stand with the rest of my cabin, just praying not to have to clean the horse shit in the stables again. I'm paying only slight attention when I hear my number being called by the overseer. I can barely believe it when he states that my team and I will be working on repairing the roof of the main hall. I hadn't expected Quinn or I to get this lucky for a good while at least, but I'll happily take what is given.

My team and I walk towards the main hall, escorted by armed guards. There are only five of us, making us a relatively important team, further emphasizing the luck I had being put into it. I had only ever been in the main hall three times before, either to clean the mess room or when I first listened to the Judge's speech on our first arrival. Strangely, it doesn't seem like the guards are leading us towards the main entrance, but rather around the side of the building. There doesn't seem to be any door that we are headed towards until I notice it: a large wooden box connected to a cable. An elevator on the exterior of the building. The guard directs me and one of my teammates, Caleb, to get inside of the box. Once we have, the cable starts to retract and, far above me, I see a counterweight begin to fall. I knew that they had electricity here in Providence because of the solar and wind farm in the southern corner, but I had no clue that they had the mechanical knowledge or resources to be able to build a construction elevator. Once I reach the top of the four-story building, I see the large mechanism behind the elevator must be operated by someone at the top in order to function, meaning that I alone couldn't use it as a way of sneaking on to the top of the hall.

Once on the roof, I could now see my true objective: the water tanks for the sprinkler systems. There were seven in total, which makes sense given the size of the building. Each one is a tall, metal cylinder with a rounded top. There are funnels coming out of the tanks that probably serve to collect rainwater, although the elevator would let them bring up water from the lake bordering the south side of Providence in the event of a drought. I don't see where the pipes connect it to the sprinkler system throughout the building. Since the cylinder connects all the way to the floor of the roof, that probably means the connection is done just below where the water is stored, but still obscured from the outside.

I must have spent too much time looking at the sprinkler tanks, because one of the guards yells at me to get a move on. I figured that we would be relaying the wooden planks on the roof or repainting something, but much to my surprise, we are escorted to one of the tanks furthest away from the elevator. Apparently, it had been struck by lightning in the last storm, so they didn't trust its structural integrity anymore. The first thing they have us do is drain the tank by connecting a hose to a valve at the tank's front end and pouring the water over the side of the building. We need a special, large wrench to be able to open the large valve, so I immediately recognize that it will be vital to our plan's success. Once that is done, the guards tell us to unscrew the blackened paneling where the lightning struck and replace it with new, undamaged panels. Once that is finished, they have us repaint the floor around where we had been working because we had scuffed and scratched it pretty badly.

They give us a short break before escorting us down to go to another job, as this only took us until a little past noon. Just as we are about to leave, I notice that the guard with the wrench puts it in a locked box on the roof with the other tools that we used. The lock looks thick, but I'm sure that ultimately it will be no obstacle to achieving our goal. The most challenging part of all of this will be getting atop the building, since the elevator can only be operated through the top. I could try to go in through the hall itself, although I'm not sure how well that would work, given how populated that area is. Trying to sneak through it would be a complete nightmare. Despite all the shit that has happened to me I give thanks that I was given this assignment, since figuring out what I have today would have been substantially more difficult without it.

Once I reach the ground, the guard informs us that our next job is to help repair the electricity farm. I am both excited and disappointed to hear this news. I think the job probably will not be too dangerous or disgusting, but I don't want to see more wonders of engineering that I will soon be destroying. When I arrive at the wind farm, I am genuinely impressed. It is far more magnificent than I expected. Massive rotating blades carve through the air with an effortless elegance. Looking at it, I almost forget the infernal purpose that the energy it creates is used for. The work I do on the windmills is menial and bland, just screwing in bolts here and there while the people that are educated in the ways of electricity do the interesting work in making sure this whole operation runs smoothly.

The man running this operation is a citizen of Providence, as the guards don't have the smarts to fix or maintain these creations of science. He's scrawny, with uncalloused hands, showing that he hasn't done any actual labor in quite a long time. His eyes aren't unkind, and I can see him looking at us - the workers - with a sense of forlorn pity. Even if he survives our planned destruction of the town, can a man like that really make it on the outside? Will my actions condemn this man to death? It's no matter. He's made his choices in life, and I've made mine. He probably doesn't deserve what's coming to him, but neither do the people that suffer and die to allow him to live. It is easy for me to blame the suffering of the workers on people like him, but does he really have any choice in the matter? Whether he is here in Providence or somewhere else, the slavery doesn't stop, but being here, he gets to live and contribute to society. I could blame it on the Judge, since he's the one that holds it together, but he just wants to see the world he once had restored, at any cost. And given the horror of this one, is that really so hard to understand? Who is at fault? Who do I get to hate? Because I do hate, I hate this place deep down to my bones.

The work goes by fast, and soon enough I'm heading back towards my cabin. I always thought that people were good at heart. There are plenty of bad apples certainly, but the human spirit? It's got to be made of our better traits, right? Providence was the last straw. I don't know what I believe now, but it certainly isn't that. As I walk through the cabin row, I peer through the door of a building two blocks down from mine. Lying on one of the beds is a frail old man, or at least an old-looking man. Around him crowd four other people from his cabin, feeding him portions of their food. I turn my head to see Quinn coming returning from his hunt, rabbit in tow. I will be eating tonight, that's something to celebrate, I suppose.

Chapter 15- Quinn

September 30

"Do you think I'm a bad person, Kayla?"

"I wouldn't say that I think you are a bad person, more that I feel that you are. You took something away from me that was so important that it left a gaping hole where my heart once was. That has to be a bad thing. And for the most part, bad people do bad things. But knowing you, seeing you here, you don't seem all that bad."

"That's fair. If you had managed to kill Ezra back there, I would have had a hard time forgiving you as well."

"What you did to my father, and by extension my sister and I, is unforgivable. There is no changing that. Despite that, I think both you and Ezra have suffered enough at our hands and the hands of Providence. So many people in this world are openly malicious. I don't think you are, and so I think the world is better with you in it. "

"Thank you, Kayla. Those words mean a lot to me."

"You're going to have a much harder time convincing Astrid though. She still wants your head on a pike."

I give an awkward chuckle and keep walking. The only sounds we hear are the fall branches crunching under our feet and the wind whistling through the trees. If it wasn't attached to something as horrible as Providence, this forest might be kind of nice. Suddenly, the seed of an idea begins to develop in my mind. No, that would be insane, I couldn't do that. Right? If I did, I should at least confirm with Ezra though, right? He would definitely say no. But that doesn't mean I shouldn't. Fuck it.

"Ezra and I are going to destroy this place in about two weeks. Do you want to help?"

"I'm sorry, what?"

"You can see it as well as I do, any worker who stays here definitely will die. There simply isn't enough food. Since I know you don't want to leave Astrid to die here, this is probably your best bet if you both want to survive. You could report us, but one month of rations won't save you for another ten months. And I have a feeling that when winter comes, food is about to become a hell of a lot more scarce."

"But if we are caught w-"

"We die if we don't."

"Astrid will help you. She hates this place even more than I do, but only if she is promised a reckoning."

"A reckoning?"

"A chance to fight and kill Ezra. She doesn't care as much about you since he was the one to pull the trigger."

"And we both agree that such a reckoning would be bad for both parties."

She shows a devilish smile before saying, "Correct."

"Then, I think we know what needs to be done."

"So tell me, how do you two plan on destroying an entire town by yourselves?"

"Well, we aren't by ourselves now, are we?"

I explain to her the general idea of our plan, specifically how we are aiming to burn down the main hall and kill the Judge in the commotion. On the topic of getting on top of the hall to release the sprinklers, she says that she's an adept climber and could probably reach the top of the building to lower the elevator. That was the last problem that I was waiting to solve, meaning now the only thing that's left is to finish smuggling in the lighters and to collect enough tinder.

The rest of the day flies by, and soon enough, it's time to return to Providence with my spoils. I decide that today's a fine day to bring back another lighter, so I head to the oak tree where it is buried and use my hands to dig it up. The small plastic box looks so mundane. To someone twenty years ago, it would just be a cheap box of lighters. To us today, it's a hope for a better future. I take out one of the five remaining lighters and place it inside the flesh of one of the rabbits that I have caught. I feel a little bad for desecrating the animal's body in such a way, but what must be done must be done.

With each passing day, the sun sets earlier and earlier, reducing the overall share of food that workers bring in. As a result, Providence has occasionally started taking shares as large as sixty percent from workers, even though doing so violates the already unfair rules that they have established. It's not like this place was already concerned with fairness though. I hide the lighter in its head, a part which they generally never take, so I assume that I will be fine no matter what. I am wrong.

The guard processing my hunt is a short, stocky man with a thick mustache but no beard. I place my kills on the blood-soaked table and wait for him to reach for the knife to cut it with, but to my surprise he just reaches to grab both rabbits and take them whole. I try to avoid confrontation with the guards as much as I possibly can. Now is one of those times when I have no other choice.

"Hey, please man, I know you guys are low on food, but can I at least have some of my hunt?"

"You want to eat, huh?"

"Yes sir, I want to eat."

"Okay, then eat," he says before slicing a piece of raw rabbit flesh and throwing it at my feet.

I grit my teeth and say, "Yes, sir."

Slowly, I pick up the piece of meat and start lowering it into my mouth. The guard is visibly shocked, whilst also being amused. He calls over to his friend to have him look at the "show" I'm putting on. The dirty meat is repulsive, with every instinct I have telling me to spit it out. But through the disgust, through the extreme discomfort, I manage to swallow it. Now I can only hope that my "show" is enough for them to give me my food back. The guard, as well as his companion within the stall burst into laughter, which as humiliating as it is, I hope is a good sign towards the prospect of retrieving my food.

"Wow, you are a funny one! You know what, keep this one," he says as he slides the rabbit with the lighter towards me.

"Thank you, sir," I reply as I snatch the rabbit from the table.

I can see that all the other workers around are staring at me. I can't tell whether it's from disgust or admiration. Maybe it's a combination of both. I hurry back towards the cabin, the revolting taste of raw meat still fresh in my mouth. I can't tell whether I should be proud of what I did or whether it is just the ultimate act of bootlicking. In any case, it doesn't really matter. I got the lighter which is what I was seeking to acquire, so I label this a success in my book. Who knows what would have happened if they found the lighter in the rabbit? Our whole plan might have been screwed.

Ezra is already back in the cabin when I arrive. He seems surprised to see me carrying in a rabbit as I enter.

"I thought that they were taking everything today. How did you manage that?"

"I'd rather not talk about it. Wanna roast it?"

He nods his head, and we go outside. I have already slid the lighter out on the way over, letting it rest in my pocket until I can access the stash. Ezra is probably going to be very mad when he learns about what I told Kayla. It's too late to change anything now and in all honesty, I don't really regret what I have done. Kayla provides the final piece of the puzzle that will help us destroy this hellhole.

"Ezra, I told Kayla and therefore Astrid by extension about our plan. They're going to help us, specifically with getting on the roof to drain the sprinkler."

Ezra sits in silence for a second before saying, "Okay, that's fine. Astrid wants to kill me herself and get out of this place too. She won't report us. Though, I imagine Astrid will only do all of this if she is somehow promised revenge against us once Providence is dealt with."

"Kayla said that Astrid will only help if she is promised a 'reckoning' with you and you alone. But we don't have to worry about that. Kayla agrees that such an encounter would be pointless, so she will help us deceive Astrid into avoiding our departure. Based on what she said, Kayla is off the path of vengeance. If Astrid wants to chase us all the way to South Bend, it will be alone."

"I guess that hopefully that will settle that. On another note, we need to re-work the specifics of how everything will go down now that we have two extra people."

"I was thinking that we should split up into pairs, you and I to kill the Judge and incite the riot, and Astrid and Kayla go to drain the sprinkler tanks and light the fire.

"That's a lot of trust we're putting in Astrid and Kayla. Without a fire, this plan fails miserably. We can't kill the Judge until the guards flee to put it out."

"Kayla is the only one of us who thinks they are capable of climbing up the hall. Either we split so you go with her, and I go with Astrid, or we do it how I said before."

"I guess we do it the first way. Trying to work with someone I've never worked with before could get complicated."

"We should probably seek them out tomorrow so we can talk to both of them about this at once."

"Sounds good."

We sit there for a little while after the food is all gone, and the plan fully discussed. When was the last time we talked about something that wasn't about getting out of here or some other logistical matter? When was the last time we just had one of our stupid arguments? I take a good look at Ezra, who is staring up at the sky with eyes that seem mostly drained of life. It's clear how much skinnier he has gotten over his time here, his muscles steadily fading since our arrival. Despite all of this, I still think that he is the most beautiful person I have ever seen.

I move over so I'm closer to him and lay my head down in his lap. He starts to run his hands through my unkempt and grown out hair, with my face pressed against his warm thigh. I love him. I really do. I haven't said it as much recently because this shithole has kept me too distracted.

"I love you," I blurt out.

"I love you too," he replies softly.

The night approaches fast and with it we are herded back into our cabin. Leaving Ezra's embrace is a dismal affair, but I know that I can enjoy it forever once we torch this place, which gives me the strength to bear it.

* * *

October 1

I approach the schoolhouse with one other worker who had just arrived in the last shipment. I never caught his name and he never offered it, as is often the case with workers of Providence. Apparently, we have to help build two new bookcases for the children here. The schoolhouse is a rare assignment, and I really had hoped that I wouldn't have to come here before the torching because I know seeing it is going to hurt me more than any other assignment could. The schoolhouse itself is a small building directly next to the main hall. It's about twice the size of the cabins we live in, with a big red door at its front, as opposed to our open entrances. The other worker and I are escorted to the door, and the guard then proceeds to knock on it.

The door opens to a short, animated woman in a long skirt. She beckons the three of us in with a smile. The inside of the schoolhouse separates into two different parts: the classroom and the library. While the woman is bringing us towards the library, I peek inside the classroom, even though I know how much it will hurt me. In fact, I do it because it will hurt me. I'm taking these kids' lives away, the least I can do is suffer a little for it. Inside the class there are kids from the ages of seven to fifteen, looking at different parts of the long blackboard at the front of the room for their specific assignment. I can see them gossiping to each other, presumably about our presence. I wonder if any of them will be able to survive once Providence is no more. I wish I could warn them, let them know what is coming so they might have a better chance to pull through. But I can't. As much as I want to, I can't.

The library is full of what seems to be around 150-200 books. The lady informs us that they are running out of space for all the books that the expeditions bring back, so they need a new shelf. The worker and I start building immediately, putting together the planks of wood with the screws that they have provided us. I scan the books out of curiosity when one piques my interest. I almost glance over it, but I don't miss that same white spine. A seemingly undamaged copy of *The Guild of Oleander* sits in the corner of the highest shelf on the bookcase to my right.

The other worker and I are busy with our task, so I can't take out the undamaged copy of the book to give to Ezra. They probably wouldn't let me take it regardless. At least I could read the end so that I could tell Ezra how it goes. While we work, the woman who let us in approaches with two cups of water. The other worker with me stands up to get the cup from her. The guard who is supposed to be watching ended up picking up a book and sitting down with it on the other side of the room, making him completely oblivious to what the worker is doing. I don't think much of what I am witnessing until the last moment, when I see the screwdriver concealed behind the man's back.

I jump up and try to grab the worker before anything can happen, screaming at the woman to try to alert her as I move. The worker makes a guttural noise as he plunges the screwdriver into the woman's neck. The water she was carrying spills out onto the floor, with the cups giving a hollow clank as they bounce across the wood. Her petite body collapses before I even get close to the worker, who has already started charging the guard in front of him. As the worker gets about five feet away from the guard, still charging like a maniac with his bloody screwdriver, the guard fires a shot directly through his skull, splattering blood across my body and the bookcase. I go to cradle the woman, putting my hand over the wound to try to stop the blood from spilling out. Despite my efforts, her blood keeps seeping through, mixing and swirling with the water coating the floor. I scream at the guard to come and help me, as he still seems to be in shock from the fact that he just killed someone. I don't even understand where all the blood is coming from until I put my hand on the back of her head and feel the warm fluid oozing out. I acknowledge the inevitable; this woman is going to die. The best I can do at this point is to hold her in her last moments.

I can hear the children in the other room screaming, likely terrified by the ruckus they have just heard. The other guard is manically searching the room for bandages or anything to help the woman, but he too has probably seen the writing on the wall. The corpse of the dead worker lays flat on the ground, empty eyed and staring at me. Am I just as bad as him? If this woman somehow lived past this, she would likely die when we torch this place. Sure, my plan will be effective in dismantling this, unlike that man's hopeless rage, but the effects will be the same. How many of the children in the other room are going to die because of my actions? How many more adults will die if I were to do nothing? There's just no winning.

I look back down to the dying woman in my arms. I can see that despite her pain, she is trying to say something. Not wanting to let her last words go unheard, I lean in close.

"Tell her I love her."

Her body goes limp in my arms. I set her down on the floor and stand up, ready to inform the guard. The half-finished bookcase, the blood-spattered books, the two dead bodies and the pool of blood and water at my feet is almost too much to bear, even given the horrid things I have seen and done.

"There's no use. She's gone."

The guard leans back against the wall and gives out a primal yell of anger and despair. All I can think is that it wasn't supposed to be like this. After a moment of silence, the guard gets up to escort the children out of the building, so they don't have to see. Since I'm all covered in blood, he tells me to wait until he returns. I look back to *The Guild of Oleander* sitting on the shelf. I could easily take it right now and check the ending but that seems... wrong, so I sit and wait, yearning for this painful ordeal to be over. In the other room, I hear the children ask questions about what's going on or where their teacher is, but the guard only responds with, "I'll tell you later."

The guard eventually returns, and we exit the schoolhouse, both of us a lot more hollow than we entered.

He tells me that I'm done working for the day and don't need to report for another assignment, so I return to my cabin and lay in my bunk. I stare at the ceiling and think. I think about where I've been, where I am, and most importantly, where I am going.

Interlude - On Freedom

No one is born free. Or lives free or dies free for that matter. From the cradle to the casket (although most people don't get those anymore) we are all enslaved. Enslaved to our wants and needs, our circumstances and our genetics. No matter how hard we try, no human will ever be able to get around these four factors. My actions will never truly be free because they are all guided by something that is out of my control. We are all just fleshy marionettes dancing across the stage of life, yet we are convinced that we are the ones in control of it all.

This is the only way to reconcile what I have seen and done, all the violence and pain and hatred. Even the most openly malicious and psychotic person didn't ask to be born that way. Why do they deserve suffering for being born with a mind that derives pleasure from other people's suffering? Why do others deserve suffering for being put in a situation where moral wrongdoing is the only way out? You could place moral wrongdoing on parents for forcing children into a world with no agency, but that doesn't work either because they were subject to the same needs, wants, circumstances, and genetics that force their children into terrible situations.

I'm not trying to say that there is no free will entirely. Honestly, I couldn't care less if there is or isn't. What I am trying to say is that it plays such a small role compared to factors outside of a person's control that it can be considered negligible. To make a comparison, a worker in Providence has free will (check previous entry for conditions in

Providence), but because of all the impositions on them, they are not free. I think that it's the same for people generally, just with the impositions being the factors I mentioned above, rather than armed guards.

We are all pieces in a cruel game where the rules are unknown, and the objectives are constantly changing. All I know is that it's pointless and wrong to hate the other pieces for being born in a way that made them do shitty things. The only malice I have left in my heart is towards the universe, God, or whatever you want to call it. The infernal engine of all the suffering in the world.

I thought, if anything, my trials would drive me further into misanthropy and distrust of humans. I was wrong. My trials have driven me not to hate humanity, but to pity it. I pity the conditions we must suffer through and the misconception that we are to blame for them. I pity the losses we endure and the despair it brings us. Most of all, I pity how we, convinced of life's wonder, perpetuate our sorry state, bringing more people into life's gnashing jaw.

-Quinn

Chapter 16- Ezra

October 14

In the distance I can see Quinn returning with spoils in hand. That's good; we are going to need to be on a full stomach for the events of tonight. I patiently await his arrival by the spot in the square where I had already prepared to make a fire. He arrives with a determined look on his face, painfully aware of the duty we have. Our meal is a quiet one, as all the plans have already been discussed and all the preparations have been made. Astrid and Kayla are to light up the main hall, and we are to assassinate the Judge.

After we eat, we go back into the cabin and await the commencement of our plan. The rest of the workers have gone to sleep, taking what little rest they are allowed in Providence.
Quinn and I are wide awake however, too energized by fear, excitement, and anxiety to dare tempt entering the land of dreams. I wonder if this is how soldiers feel right before they go into battle. Many people are going to die tonight. Even when I think those words, they don't seem true. This isn't like the other times I have killed. No, this is premeditated. I have decided that my will is more important than the life of others. That isn't exactly the truth either. This is just a matter of numbers, isn't it? Killing the few to save the many? That's another lie, isn't it? I care about the workers from a mental standpoint, but they aren't why I'm doing this. I'm doing this for Quinn and I'm doing this for me. I have to right this world's wrong, despite what I have to pay to do it.

I see Quinn signal to me from above. Through the crack in the roof, he can see that the moon is midway across the sky, our agreed upon time for our operation to start. Now comes the first tricky part of the plan, which is getting out of our cabin without alerting any of the other workers. They should all be in a very deep sleep, and even if they aren't, they should know better than to try to stop us. I tiptoe out of my bed, and help Quinn get down with as little noise as possible. Nobody seems to have jolted awake, which is a good first sign. The two of us sneak out the open door, careful to minimize the noise coming from the cabin's creaky floorboards. Due to the nature of our job, I leave the *Guild of Oleander* behind, but I am still grateful to have read it one last time.

Now we have worked in enough time to wait and see if any of the other workers in our cabin awoke and are going to tell someone about our betrayal. There are plenty of guard patrols around this area, but from our observations on previous nights, they tend to stay near the walls and around the perimeter of the worker housing area, rather than inside of it. Still, just waiting out here in the open is not something that I want to be doing for longer than I need. After about seven minutes, I pester Quinn to get going, but he shakes his head. We decided to wait ten minutes and so that is what we will do.

Just as the ninth minute approaches, we hear footsteps coming out of the cabin. Both of our eyes go wide, and we position ourselves on both sides of the open door so we can snatch the guy right when he steps out. Quinn plants his hand over his mouth and pushes him to the ground and I restrain his arms and keep him from thrashing. I've spoken to him before a few times; his name's Finn, I think. Both of us move him away from the cabin in an effort to avoid waking anyone else up.

"I'm going to move my hand off your mouth now. If you scream, we will kill you immediately."

Finn nods his head, so Quinn removes his hand.

"I wasn't going to snitch on you guys, I was just trying to make my own escape in the pandemonium that your escape will cause."

"And you left your partner in the cabin because...?"

Quinn sees that he is probably going to scream so he covers Finn's mouth before he can. It's clear as day that this man wanted to snitch. If he wanted to escape without his partner, he would have just left on a hunt. The men with female partners are in a different cabin, so that can't be a solution.

Blood erupts from Finn's neck as Quinn's knife pierces into it. I look at him completely aghast. This man did not deserve death. He was just trying to provide for himself and his partner. The Judge, now that is someone that has brought on what is coming to him, but this is just cold-blooded murder. A part of me is glad that Quinn did what he did, because we had no other way of preventing this man from snitching and spoiling the entire plan. But the speed, the lack of hesitation that he showed disturbs me.

I shift my body to avoid being covered in the blood of the dying man. I have nothing to say to Quinn. He made the utilitarian decision, one that hopefully will be able to end the suffering of hundreds more workers. Still, I can't help but wonder, what happened to the gentle man I used to know who didn't even want to kill wild animals?

Once the worker had made his final dying gasps, we pick up and toss his body into the dumpster a few yards away from our cabin. We have no time to dawdle, since we already waited longer than we were supposed to. The path to reach the Judge's manor is relatively clear, since most of the guards are used to keeping us in rather than stopping our movement within Providence. The manor is a large, walled wooden house sitting on the highest point in Providence, with a nice garden stretching out in front of it, and four guards positioned outside of it that are in clearly illuminated positions on the patio. We sit crouching outside of the manor's walls, waiting to see the burning glow of the main hall up in flames, inviting us to our target.

A pit of anxiety begins to build in my stomach. They should have lit the fire by now, especially since we had that distraction before we left. What if they got caught? Should Quinn and I just try to leave? Abandon all these people to suffer here and let the people that are causing it go unpunished? Quinn taps my shoulder and points at the left corner of the main hall. It's small, but I can clearly see a fire beginning to blaze. Now all that's left is to wait for the guards to notice it. My heart is throbbing in my chest, overcome by the crushing importance of what we are doing here. I picture the Judge's face and imagine the catharsis I would gain from ending that smug grin.

The fire begins to burn brighter, enough for it to call attention to the guards. Three of them start running off in the direction of the fire, while the last one draws his rifle and stands vigilant over the garden. Quinn and I hop on top of the wall surrounding the manor's garden. Neither of us have any firearms because we couldn't figure out how to smuggle one, so we somehow need to trick that guard to move away from the main entrance. We could try to sneak into the manor through one of the windows, but that wouldn't remove the threat of the guard entering the manor if he hears commotion.

"I've got an idea," Quinn says to me with a solemn tone.

Without even telling me what his idea is, he leaps down into the garden, sprints out from the darkened corner where he was hiding, and starts yelling.

"We need help! The fire is destroying the main hall please! Judge, we need your help!" he shouts.

Quinn collapses at the end of his speech, causing the guard to move off the patio with his weapon drawn and say,

"Who are you? How did you get in here?"

"The burns, please you have got to help me. It burns, *please!*" Quinn cries, the pain in his voice seeming unmistakably real.

With this the guard's speed increases, but he doesn't take the point of his rifle off Quinn's body. As the guard approaches, Quinn keeps wailing in pain on account of his imaginary injuries, clearly disturbing the guard. Time is running out, because if the guard gets too close, he will notice Quinn's lack of injuries and uncover his deception. I decide to leap down and start approaching the guard from behind in case whatever plan Quinn has doesn't pan out. However, as I sneak towards the guard's position, Quinn pulls his dagger from under him and flings it into the guard's chest in one smooth motion. The guard releases a barrage of fire from his assault rifle, but they all go wide. I start sprinting and grab him from behind before he has time to take aim once more. Quinn leaps up and pulls his knife out of the man's chest and slits his throat with it. I pick up the man's rifle, and we both start sprinting into the house, trying to avoid giving the Judge time to prepare, since he is now alert to our presence.

The interior of the manor is unlit, but we can still see the fine western style design that went into making this place: hide rugs, well-crafted furniture, and even picture frames showing what looks to be Tobias before the rapture, dressed in a camo outfit embroidered with an American flag. We don't see movement in the main hall, so we head up the staircase to the second floor. Stalking down the hall, we hear a banging noise coming from the room at the end of the hall. I expect Tobias is hunkered down in there, shotgun pointed at the door, just waiting for us to burst in. Wanting to avoid being sawed in two the second I open the door, I give Quinn a look of warning, so he knows to be prepared for what's to come. I unleash a barrage of bullets through the door before I kick open the shattered remains and sprint in.

Surprisingly, I find no blood, no corpse, and even no weapon. What I do find is a woman curled up in the corner on the other side of the room holding a screaming toddler. Neither Quinn nor I have any idea of what to do at this point. Both of us agreed that we must be ruthless to destroy this place, but harming an innocent woman and child is beyond what we are capable of.

"Please don't hurt my baby, please, I'm begging you, please don't," the woman cries.

"Just tell us where Tobias is, and we will leave you alone. That's all we want to know," Quinn says calmly with his knife brandished in his hand.

"No, no, no, you can't hurt him. He said not to say anything."

"We don't want to hurt you, but if you don't tell us where he is you leave us no choice. I see your kid right there. If you don't want anything to happen to them, you are going to have to speak up. *Now.*"

"I can't. I just can't. Leave, please just leave me alone!" she screams while holding her child close to her chest so they can't see or hear what's going on.

Quinn crouches down and looks into her eyes before saying, "I know this is hard, but you have to tell us. Unless you want your kid to die, we need to know where Tobias is."

Tears flow from the woman's eyes uncontrollably. Her eyes are red and on her face is a look of pure anguish. I know that Quinn wouldn't actually hurt the kid, but from the way he said what he said I almost doubted that for a second.

"He's at the main hall overseeing a construction project. Now *leave!*"

"If you are lying, we are going to come for you. If you aren't, know that you made the right choice for your child."

The two of us are already on our way out before she can respond. I feel absolutely disgusting after that interaction, like I'm worse than human. I have always been willing to do what's necessary for Quinn, but this, this is just too much. It can't be right. There must be a better way than this. But deep down I know this is the only way. To live is to suffer. To try to end that suffering is to cause more. No, that isn't true. What's wrong is this world. It's broken and any attempt at fixing it only breaks it more.

"Come on, we have to get there fast. Astrid and Kayla should have already left by now, meaning it's up to us if we want to kill Tobias," Quinn says to me, noticing me losing focus.

"Yeah, got it."

"Keep your head in the game. We are almost done with all this."

I nod and do my best to refocus. He's right. After the Judge is gone, Providence is done. Up ahead I can see the blaze spreading from the main hall onto the other buildings surrounding it. Still, I know that my greatest trial of the night will come once this is all over.

As we approach, I can feel the immense heat emanating off the burning building. If the Judge is in there, he is as good as dead. But perhaps he is leading a firefighting effort on the periphery of the building. The workers should already have started running off by now, so even if he does manage to stop the fire, Providence would be in dire straits, yet I can't leave something like that up to chance. And regardless, all the workers of Providence deserve justice. Tobias shouldn't be able to pack up and move on after what he has done. As we run around the border of the burning building, we see guards, workers, and citizens all running frantically as it all comes crashing down.

I see a woman standing right in front of the wall of flame engulfing the building screaming a guttural cry. I listen closer and realize that she is screaming a person's name. Suddenly, her scream is cut short by a burning wooden beam that breaks from the rest of the structure and comes crashing down directly on top of the woman. Turning my head away before I witness her death, I am left to imagine the horror of her mangled body. Her death only strengthens my resolve. My penance for all of this will come, but until then I must finish what I started.

The sounds of Providence collapsing all around us are a cacophony of crackling fire, screams of despair, and occasional gunfire as guards try to maintain order. I wonder if this is what it was like when society collapsed back in the rapture. Is it just our nature to start killing each other once things start to go south? No, that isn't right. We just try to protect what we have, even if that means taking from others. I can't think about this right now, I need to focus.

I grip my rifle tighter to calm my nerves. The heat from the fire all around us is causing me to sweat heavily. Quinn and I have almost travelled around the entirety of the main hall when we notice about five men taking buckets of water from the trough of the stable next to the main hall and throwing it onto the raging fire. It's such a pitiful display that I don't think much of it until I glance at the side profiles of one of the men. To my shock, I recognize the outline of the Judge. Without even thinking, I point my rifle at the man's back and hold down the trigger. A volley of bullets tears into his back, causing a cry of pain to erupt from the pathetic looking man. He falls flat towards the building and the flames begin to lick at his dying body. The other men start running for cover at the sound of gunfire, leaving the scene completely empty after just a few moments.

It doesn't even feel real right away. I had done what I had been aiming to accomplish since the moment I arrived here. But there isn't any satisfaction, any absolution, any long monologue where our opponent tries to justify what he did. I didn't get a suspenseful, dramatic fight where I best the villain through skill, determination, and righteousness. I didn't get any release of all the pent-up hatred I had in store. What I did was kill a man that seemed as helpless as we were when first captured. The Judge is dead, and Providence has fallen. We have won, but it seems… hollow.

"Come on, we have to get out of here unless we want to end up like him," Quinn says before starting off, heading north.

"Alright, but I already mapped the best way out of here a few days ago, follow me."

Quinn changes direction and accepts my request, although he does give a minor expression of confusion, likely over why I hadn't brought this up before. As we jog away from the heart of Providence, the sounds of screaming and violence begin to fade, but still leave their disturbing mark in the distance. As we pass by one of the corpses of a guard, Quinn leans down and picks up the dead man's rifle. I figure that will be useful to help us survive once we are back in the wild, given that he doesn't have any other tools besides his knife. The imposing wall of Providence looms above us. Normally, there would be guards stationed all along its rim, but tonight it is completely empty. We climb up the wooden stairs on one side and walk along the wall for a few hundred feet looking for a ladder down to the opposite side.

We find it and lower it down so that it touches the earth on the other side of the wall. Before I leave, I level my gaze towards the town behind the wall. From this viewpoint, I can see almost all of Providence. The fire in the main hall has spread to almost the entire central area, and even seems to have spread to the worker cabins on the opposite side of the main hall. I know I will never return here, so with one final look, I bid Providence goodbye, turn my head, and climb down the ladder.

Once we are at the bottom, I start to take Quinn through a path worn by many of the workers that used to come through here. He seems a little suspicious of why we are heading west when our destination is to the north. Still, he trusts me enough not to make a fuss about it, which is what matters right now. After a minute or two of walking, the sounds of Providence fade, leaving only the chirping of crickets and the cool whistling of the wind. The night is cold, and neither Quinn nor I are dressed for it. Still, I must press on for just a little bit longer. I look up towards the glowing moon that hangs in the sky - the same moon I looked at on that night before everything went to shit. That's one constant I know I can believe in. As long as there is an earth, that moon will hang in the sky, whether I am here or not.

Without even realizing it, I now stand at the base of the largest oak tree in the vicinity, with its arms branching out for hundreds of feet. I guess this is it then. Knowing what is to come, I quickly turn to Quinn and kiss him on his sweet and perfect lips. While telling him that I love him, I then walk a few feet away. Astrid and Kayla emerge swiftly from the brush. Kayla knocks Quinn down in a surprise attack and, despite his larger size, she can place her knee on his neck and restrain him fully. I can see the surprise and betrayal in his eyes, and that pains me more than anything else. I look straight ahead of me towards Astrid's silhouette and notice a hammer clutched tightly in her right hand. I fall to my knees and give Quinn a forced smile. He starts to scream, with the beginnings of the word "why" forming before Kayla stuffs a piece of cloth into his mouth. Tears begin to build in the corners of my eyes. This really is it for me. I look up at Astrid's face clenched with a cool rage, likely reliving the moments of pain she feels every time she longs for her father.

"Remember the deal," I tell her, trying to keep my voice from wavering.

"I will."

I had always known I was going to die, but I never thought it was going to be so soon. I had thought that one day Quinn and I would be able to live together as we truly wanted, but it was not meant to be. Looking in the face of my death, I regret nothing and hope only that Quinn finds the strength to go on without me.

Crack.

Interlude - Goodbye

I love you, Quinn. Before anything else you just need to know that I love you, more than anything. I may be gone from the physical world, but my memory, my "spirit" if you will, lives. Those memories that we share, nothing can take that away from them, not death, not suffering, not anything. So I beg of you, don't let that memory die out. Whatever you do, you just have to live. I know it sounds hypocritical coming from me, but please, it's my last wish.

You want absolution, I know. But the truth is that I can't give it to you because you didn't do anything wrong, at least to me. I did what I did because it was the only way to ensure your safety without giving up what was left of my humanity. I've thought about all the people that have died because I decided to be stupid and try to play the hero that June morning. They deserve this. They deserve for the architect of their despair to face some kind of justice. I never wanted it to be like this. Trust me, the only thing I wanted was to spend the rest of my life with you. But I just can't. This weight, it must be satisfied.

I can only hope that Astrid will choose to spare me, and you will never have to read this letter, but in my heart, I know that it won't be so. I have taken something immeasurable from her. That leaves a debt that can only be paid back in something immeasurable. I know you will want revenge from her, but please don't take it. End this cycle of violence.

I've thought a lot about the *Guild of Oleander* in the past few days. I think it's better that I don't know the ending, because it means I get to decide on my own. Knowing what type of book, it is, it probably has some way for Archeon to avoid the question entirely. But I think that question is important, and one you might have to face in the coming months. Are you willing to be responsible for all that man does after Sin? I can't tell you what to do, because well, it isn't my world anymore. Let's just say that I know what ending I would have given to the story.

In my death I will find peace. I know how hard this is going to be for you, but please do not hold on to that pain for too long. For the first time in a long time, I will soon know no pain, no suffering, and no worldly burdens. I will get the rest I was denied during my stay on Earth.

In spite of everything, I am still glad to have lived, and even more glad that I lived with you. I want you to know that to me, you are the strongest, smartest, most wonderful person that ever has or will walk this Earth. My time here is over, but yours is just beginning. This I can promise.

Forever and Eternally Yours,
Ezra

Chapter 17- Quinn

December 2

I lower Ezra's final note back into my back pocket, staining the corner with a teardrop as I do. 201 Chapin St, South Bend, IN 46601. After all the trials I have endured since we set out months ago, I made it. Even so, standing here alone, I feel not triumph, but a hollowness. It wasn't supposed to be like this. We were supposed to make it here together. He is supposed to be standing by my side when we reach the conclusion of all of this. I look to my right, into the space where he should be standing, but see only empty air and a deserted road. At a time like this he would make some witty comment, maybe I would look into his eyes, and we would have a good laugh, something like that. But now, there isn't the warmth of his voice or the brightness of his smile, just the bitter December cold and a desolate, decaying street.

Despite the hole in my being that is threatening to render me unable to function, I know that I must press on. At least for a little bit. All we have done has been in search of this, and I must see what it has to offer. The building stands out due to its size and blocky structure, given the suburban environment that surrounds it. I stalk around the building for a few minutes, trying to find the best entrance. On my walk, I discover a faded plaque that denotes the building as a history museum. Ichthys certainly had a way of picking their hiding spots. On one side of the building, I see a few large glass windows and decide that they will probably be my best bet for gaining entry to the building. The doors appear to be too securely locked for me to gain access without expending too much energy.

I take the butt of my rifle and slam it into the glass panel. Multiple cracks spread throughout the surface of the glass, but it still holds strong. I swing one more time and again more cracks form, but the glass holds. Finally, on my third attempt, the window completely shatters, sending shards of sharp glass flying everywhere. Thankfully, none of it seems to have pierced my skin. I climb in through the space where the window once was to find a bare hall that transitions between exhibits. I follow the hall for a little while until I reach a room that opens the space up significantly. There are far fewer windows in here, so I pull out the flashlight I scavenged and take a look at what the room holds. Dozens of vintage cars litter the exhibit with little plaques explaining the make and model of each one. Seems this place was completely untouched by the collapse. Well, not completely. Many of the cars seem slightly out of shape, given the fact that they haven't seen any attention in over a decade, but this nice, enclosed environment seems to have cared for them nicely.

I search the room for hidden trap door that will let me access a basement but find nothing. I continue on my way through another hallway leading out of this room and into the main lobby of the museum. The lobby is plain, with a few non-functioning TV screens over the central desk that at one point described the price of admission. I intensify my search for some kind of hidden door, feeling the ground all throughout the entire lobby to see if there is a hidden nook. I find none. This can't be. It must be here, if the entrance were to be in any room it would be the lobby. And if it's not in the lobby it's not here. Ezra would know what to do. I'm just sure of it.

I sit for a moment and try to calm myself down. I may be alone, but I know that I can do this. Realizing I haven't fully checked the desk, I head over to that area and start feeling its underside for hidden button or lever. My fingertips find only the smooth underside of the desk. On the left side, I see a space for some drawers. I pull each and every one of them out. They seem to be completely empty, likely drained of whatever contents they had when the Rapture came. Just to be safe, I feel the bottoms of every drawer. On the last drawer, I notice that the bottom paneling has more give than the other when I apply weight. I push down on it hard, and the panel becomes completely loose. I pull it out and place it on the table, now clearly seeing the button that it was obscuring.

Upon pushing down on the button, rows of the tile floor fold up and back, revealing a staircase. To think that some hourly employee stood next to that button for days on end and never even realized what was there. As I get closer to the staircase, I can see that it is dimly lit by a row of blue LEDs, meaning that somehow this place still has emergency power. I creep down the metal staircase towards a room that is completely black. After aiming my flashlight into the darkness, I see that it is just a hallway leading straight ahead. When I reach the foot of the stairs, I scan the surrounding surfaces with my light, so I have a better idea of what this area looks like. On the wall next to me, I notice a large lever switch and decide to push it up. Upon doing so, lights all throughout the hall begin to power up, clearly illuminating the entire space.

Nobody seems to be here. What happened to the people of this Ichthys facility? Did they run out of food supply? Did they give up and leave? Suddenly, the idea of there actually being vaccine here appears to be incredibly remote. Nonetheless, I press on, walking down the metallic and sterile hallway. The end of it opens into a large, illuminated underground atrium, similar to the one that we encountered back in Colorado. I turn the handle to one of the doors on the top floor, noticing a lack of inscription denoting whose lab it was. Upon entering the room, the reason for this becomes clear. The walls that used to separate each person's lab had been taken down, making the entire space one large circular lab circumscribing the atrium. I guess since this was the place where all the research from the different labs was being put together, it made sense to try to have it be focused on collaboration. I look at all the different desks and screens and notice how they all seem carefully organized and put together. It doesn't seem like the researchers all left in a hurry or a surprise catastrophe occurred. Whatever caused this place's abandonment was slow.

I came here for answers, didn't I? I start searching the desks for papers or research on the origin of Sin, but all I find are technical documents full of complex biological words that I don't understand. Instead of Sin, they use that same word RIAA to describe the cause of the rapture. I flip to the back of the paper to see if there is a glossary of some sort, anything that would tell me what RIAA stands for. On the back page of a paper titled "On Potential Counteragents to RIAA" I discover the author uses the words "Rapid Intrinsic Apoptosis Agent (RIAA)" before talking about an mRNA-based counteragent. Those words don't mean much to me, but at least it's something. I probably won't understand much by pouring through these papers, so I decide to try to turn on one of these computers to see if they have any visuals.

To my surprise, the computer begins to power up when I press the on button. However, I am met with a user login screen for one Dr. Genovese. I scour around the desk to see if the researcher left their password anywhere, although my hopes aren't that high. To my surprise, in the left drawer there is a sticky note denoting the password as "Thickney1970." I type it in letter by letter, and press enter, causing the computer to open to its home screen. I haven't ever used a real computer like this before, but it's intuitive so I get the hang of it quickly.

I see one folder titled RIAA and click on it, finding dozens of subfolders such as data, counteragents, general research, and most importantly for me, pictures/videos. The first thing that comes up are hundreds of pictures of what used to be people, but have now just been reduced to a puddle of oozing puss. I've seen people eat something with Sin, but seeing all these pictures is really testing my will. Near the bottom of the folder, I find a video titled "Release.mov." I click on it, and it shows security camera footage in another atrium style building similar to this one. There are several figures in full hazmat suits moving around a large metallic ball that has a blue glow emitting from slanted slits running along the surface of the sphere. One of the researchers brushes his arm against the sphere, seemingly accidentally. Suddenly, there is a flash of light, and every researcher in the room is reduced to a puddle. Whatever this thing is, it's the source of Sin. I watch the video again to be sure, and it only confirms my suspicions. That orb is not of human design.

I go back to the first page of the RIAA and click on another folder titled the "Egg of Lilith," which I can only assume refers to the metal sphere. I open the first document I see, but each and every line on it has been completely redacted. Just to be sure, I look at the other files in this folder and find that they have all received the exact same treatment. Whoever was last to log in clearly did not want anyone to know anything more about the Egg. Despite my curiosity, that's something I am okay with. What I have seen settles it; Sin was not deployed by humans. I try looking in any of the other folders for more information, but all the text has received the same redacted treatment. Whether it was God or something else we can't understand who placed that orb here. I don't know, but I don't think I will be able to find much more information on this computer regardless.

I stand up and decide to head to search the next lowest floor for any information on counteragent production. This floor seems to be based on research, not production, so I think that I might have better luck if I continue my descent. As I walk down the concrete steps, a memory of me almost falling down the stairs at the facility in Colorado floods my mind. How the hell were we so goddamn happy? We had almost just died. And yet because of him, it was worth it. Living was… good…

The lab on the second floor is very similar to the one on the third in terms of design. However, scattered all throughout the lab are various pieces of machinery that I can't hope to recognize. In the immediate area where I enter, the neatness that I had witnessed on the floor above is not present here. It looks as if someone had thrown a tantrum, scattering papers everywhere, even going as far as to smash a computer against the floor. I try to read some of the papers riddled about, but they are incomprehensible to me. I don't even know what I am searching for anymore. If the people here even made an effective counteragent, they would have released it, and Sin would be over. Seeing that they haven't, there must not be any here. And even if I did find it, I don't even know what I would do with it. It was always the goal, the objective to end all of this, but feeling how I feel and knowing what I know, that seems wrong too.

I decide to walk around the rest of this floor anyway. I'm here, so I might as well see what there is to see. I check the desks as I pass, looking for a log or just anything that isn't technical jargon, but my search comes up empty. This place seems so different from anywhere else I've been. It's a true preservation of what the world once was. Not a rotting husk of it, but a true instance of the past world preserved in amber. Despite its sterile atmosphere, I wouldn't mind staying here if I had food supply.

As I continue around the circular laboratory, I see a large machine that is making a steady whirr. In front of it sits an empty wheelchair. No, it's not empty. On the seat there is a lab coat, pants, glasses, and even underwear. All of them have a large pink stain covering their entire surface. Directly in front of the wheelchair, there are black shoes and socks as well as a stapled stack of papers. What happened here is clear, but why? Did this researcher accidentally ingest Sin? How could that even happen? I imagine most of their food was pre-stored. I pick up the stack of papers on the floor and flip to its first page.

3/4/8
Production of the first prototypes of
the counteragent is finally starting to get
underway. We have lost communication with
the fifth branch, but the others are still
in contact. Our food stores should last
five years, at the least, given our current
staffing. I am hopeful that we will be able
to produce a final version of the
counteragent before then. God, I never
thought my life was going to turn out like
this, but if I can even contribute in the
slightest to saving humanity, I will do it
happily.
      - Dr. Kantz

I try to see if I can get any closer to when it all went
to shit. I flip ahead a few dozen pages and start reading.

10/6/10
The counteragents we have synthesized
should be working. It doesn't make any
sense. But after one hour, any effects that
it should be having at countering RIAA
start to wear off. We have been working at
it for months, but we still can't find a
way to prolong its protection. Not to
mention the fact that we need to find a way
to disperse it, because we don't have
enough resources to manufacture enough
counteragent for everyone on earth, even if
its effects were permanent. The entire

first floor is now being dedicated to dispersion.
          - Dr. Kantz

Even if they only made a counteragent that was effective for about an hour, it could still be useful to me if I applied it just before I ate. Only one way to find out.

          2/22/11
          Tensions are starting to run high after so many months without progress. The dispersion team has seen some success in manufacturing a system that would alter the counteragent so it could spread in a way similar to RIAA, protecting each human that consumes it. However, the current state of the counteragent is too short lived for this process to work. It just seems impossible. Every step we try leads to absolutely nothing changing. And these days of nothing are just crushing morale. Combined with the fact that all branches but the fourth have gone dark by now… The people here know we are humanity's last hope. It's too much of a burden for any of us to bear.

          - Dr. Kantz

I quickly turn to an entry about a year down the line, eager to see how it all played out.

5/16/12
I just need more time. I can figure
it out. I have to. But I just need more
time. Food supply gives us one more year at
best, but I just don't think that is going
to be enough. After four went dark, I
started hearing whispers. Whispers of
abandoning the facility and trying to make
our way out in the wastes. They know that
I couldn't come with them, so they have
been sure to be quiet. They can't give up
yet. I won't let them. Not when we still
have so much more work to do.
     - Dr. Kantz

Stuck in this enclave of civilization I can't imagine
thinking of leaving it unless it was necessary. Although I
suppose these closed walls would influence the mind after a
time.

4/1/13
They are gone. I can't believe it.
They came up to me, all of them, and told
me they were going to leave immediately so
I would have the remaining food supply to
make it a bit longer. How could they?
Abandon the work we have given our lives to
maraud around a world that our organization
helped destroy? Just when we were on the
precipice of fixing it, of healing the
broken world. Now this place is even more
hollow and soulless than it once was.

But my work is not done. My work will not be done until my very last breath leaves my body. The dispersion device is complete, so all I need to do is make the counteragent effective and then this nightmare will be over. Oh, I will show them, on the day when my colleagues find that RIAA is gone, they will wish they too could have bathed in the glory of saving mankind.

    - Dr. Kantz

She seems to be going a bit off the deep end at this point, but who wouldn't, given her circumstances. She struggles so much for the chance that humanity will suffer for a few hundred more years. And yet I cannot condemn her for I feel that same urge to keep my species going. B I flip to the last entry in the stack.

1/5/14

I figured it out. It works. It actually works. And yet I must weep. The ingredient, what I was missing, was time. We were synthesizing the counteragent over days, when what it really needed was years. Unfortunately for me, I have a few days' supply of food if I ration it heavily. And without me, a synthesized counteragent can't be transported to the dispersion device. Isn't that just comical? The one thing separating humanity from its salvation is a two-minute walk. If there is a god, he certainly loves to toy with us.

I will not sit here and waste away, however. I will die with dignity, in the way I should have on that one Sunday morning. Helen, Claire, I promise I'm coming to you soon. If by some miracle someone comes by this station, or if my colleagues ever return, just take one vial of the counteragent out of the synthesizer and place it in the dispersion device on the first floor. This will be my last entry. Goodbye.

- Dr. Kantz

I reach down into the wheelchair and pick up a metal earring in the shape of a bird perching on a branch. I will remember you, Dr. Kantz. I walk over to the synthesizer and press a large green button, causing a glass door to open. A tray holding ten vials of a blue liquid emerges from the large machine. My mind flashes back to that fateful moment when Astrid bashed in Ezra's head with that hammer before vanishing into the forest, leaving me to sob over his lifeless body. Visions of the boy being left to die on the execution stage back at Providence, the man that we saw crucified near Des Moines, flood my mind. The eyes of the teacher I held in my arms while she died pierce me now, months later.

I snatch two vials of the counteragent, one for me, and one for Ezra. Then, before I even realize what I am doing, I swing my rifle off my shoulder and smash the remaining 8 vials of the counteragent with the butt of my weapon. The sound of cracking glass hangs in the air as drops of the blue liquid fall from the extended tray onto the tile floor, each one representing another hope for humanity's future dying. In laying waste to the counteragent, a part of me rages and a part of me celebrates.

I start to walk to the door, but something calls me back. One might call it hope; hope that everything I've come to believe is wrong. What I would be doing is effectively murder. Millions of people are going to starve and die if I make this choice. God, I wish Ezra could have just told me what he wanted and made this decision easy. I head down to the lowest floor to look at the dispersion device without yet committing to use it. It's a large metal machine with a tube connecting into the wall of the facility, with a space the perfect size for a vial of the counteragent on top. I now hold the largest decision that one human has ever had to make within my hands all because some raiders decided to attack our village months ago. I'm not qualified for this. I have my ideals, but what if there is something I am missing? If I could give everyone the counteragent without letting humanity expand, I wouldn't hesitate, but I can't be complicit in the creation and suffering of billions of more humans. Even if one day they would re-establish a world that is far less cruel than the one of today, all the pain that would come between now and then would be *my* responsibility. How many more slaves would be born, suffer, and die as humanity climbs that ladder back to civilization? How many more settlements like Providence would grow until we escape the kill or be killed mentality that dominates this world?

Ezra always wanted to help people; it's how I ended up in this place to begin with. He said that this is my choice to make, but is this really what he would have wanted? For just a second, I consider lowering the vial into the slot. I consider saving the lives of hundreds of millions of human beings. But right before I do, I remember that one line in his note. "It isn't my world anymore."

He wouldn't have wanted this. For me to sacrifice my ideals for some flawed conception of who he was. Ezra can't be summed up as a man who 'wanted to help people.' He was and always will be so much more than that. He was brilliant, reckless, kind, and willful. He was everything I could have ever wanted. And he wouldn't want me to make humanity continue to suffer to fulfill some vague idea of saving the world in his memory.

I take the vials in my pocket and ascend the concrete stairs with nothing holding me back and nothing to prop me up if I fall. I am free.

Epilogue

I kneel in front of a carved stone with Ezra's name on it at the base of the largest oak tree for miles. Behind me stands a wooden cabin that I have constructed from the rubble of our former prison. I never thought that I would return to Tennessee, but I couldn't bear the idea of Ezra laying in an unmarked grave. From this spot, the ruins of Providence are not visible, which is the only reason I can stand being in such proximity. Nevertheless, being so close to it gives me a calm sense of forlorn longing for the days Ezra and I spent there. Oh, how we hated them, and what I would give to get them back.

In my pocket I feel the comfortable weight of the vials of counteragent that I have kept on my person up until today. I look next to me at the smaller grave of Dr. Kantz, whose earring I buried below a smaller rock in which I carved her name. Cruel irony, isn't it? Her ghost about to witness the last of her life's work be poured down the figurative drain. I like to think that her spirit has left this world, dining on an eternal feast with Helen and Claire, whoever they are.

I feel the familiar brush of Umbra as her fur slides against my leg. Her companionship will never rival that of Ezra's, but she does manage to make living like this considerably less lonely. When I first saw her wandering the burnt-out ruins of Providence, I knew her to be a kindred spirit. She lets out a low purr as I brush my hand over her head. How I would have loved for Ezra to meet her.

Ezra has been the pillar of my life for as long as I can remember. His voice, the very comfort of his presence is what made this world bearable for me. Looking up at the moon, I remember the pointless banter that we would have while lying in our sleeping bags, back when we were still so full of hope towards the world that we were going to change. It was a different time, a better time. But it was that same time that we struggled against the rage that stemmed from our own actions.

Astrid and Kayla are gone, and I have no intention of pursuing them. Ezra made his choice and, as much as it pains me, I have to accept it. My days of fighting are over. If someone comes seeking retribution for someone I have killed, I have no intention of denying them. Until then, I intend to live how Ezra wanted me to live.

The night is silent, much like it was during our stay in Providence. I often wonder how many of those workers made it out of Providence, and how many are still alive today. Despite what I had to do and how many died because of it, I know that those workers will have better lives than they ever could have under Providence. The ruined city is truly Ezra's legacy. I never learned the details of his deal with the sisters, but the outcome was clear. Without them, there is no way that Providence ever could have been destroyed. He never got to know what lay at the end of our journey, but he died accomplishing something that was the essence of everything he was and believed in. I could never have been more proud of him.

I wonder if I will ever house a passing stranger in my humble abode much like Doug did for us. One day, I will go visit him and tell him all that transpired. He is probably one of the only remaining people that ever truly got to meet Ezra, even if our departure was not on the friendliest of terms.

One of the first things that I did upon my return to Providence was search the old schoolhouse to see if the *Guild of Oleander* somehow survived the fire. I searched through the pile of destroyed books and identified its stark white cover, but the pages had all been charred. I was never able to read this story that meant so much to Ezra, but perhaps that is for the best. Ezra's descriptions of the narrative will stick with me until the moment of my death.

Now to the matter at hand. I reach into my pocket and pull out the vials of the counteragent. I stare into that swirling blue liquid and contemplate all the actions that have led to this moment. Humanity will die and all this suffering will end. For this I rejoice. As I pour the liquid on to his grave I whisper,

"Ezra, we did it. We found the cure together."

Acknowledgements

I would like to thank William Olrich and Julia Krawiecki-Gazes for carefully helping me turn the mess that was my first draft into a fully developed novel. They have been a massive boon to the story and have shaped it into what it is today. Ava Levine deserves the utmost recognition for the wonderful work she has done in crafting the spectacular cover art; I am truly lucky to have her skills. My patient mentor, Tyrone Sandaal, is the person who made this work possible. Without him and his everlasting dedication to encouraging me and my writing, I doubt I would have had the courage or motivation to embark on this journey. My loving parents, Christine Barney and Robert Gill, have supported me in every stage of this process. Their words, their time, and their generosity fueled my creative energy and intellectual interest. Their contribution to this work is ineffable. My sister, Alexa Bishopric, has cultivated my curiosity and encouraged my growth ever since I was born. She has done so much to make me the person that could write this book.

Writing a book is rarely a solitary process, and in my case it certainly wasn't. There are far more people that I could name that played a role in this book's development, but in truth if I went down that road, I would have to name almost everyone I had ever met. This book is a product of who I am today, and that person only exists because of the many people who have been there along the way. To all of you, thank you. My final thanks goes out to you, the reader, for indulging me with your time.

www.ingramcontent.com/pod-product-compliance
Lightning Source LLC
Chambersburg PA
CBHW031717170626
46808CB00005B/1789